RUSTLERS' RANGE

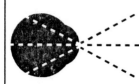

RUSTLERS' RANGE

BRADFORD SCOTT

WHEELER PUBLISHING
A part of Gale, Cengage Learning

GALE
CENGAGE Learning

Detroit • New York • San Francisco • New Haven, Conn • Waterville, Maine • London

GALE
CENGAGE Learning

LIBRARY OF CONGRESS CATALOGING-IN-PUBLICATION DATA

Scott, Bradford, 1893–1975.
    Rustlers' range / by Bradford Scott.
      p. cm. — (Wheeler Publishing large print western)
    ISBN-13: 978-1-4104-1840-1 (pbk. : alk. paper)
    ISBN-10: 1-4104-1840-5 (pbk. : alk. paper)
    1. Large type books. I. Title.
PS3537.C9265R87 2009
813'.54—dc22   2009015930

Published in 2009 by arrangement with Golden West Literary Agency.

Printed in the United States of America
1 2 3 4 5 6 7 13 12 11 10 09

CAST OF CHARACTERS

Jim Woodard, range detective. He came to solve a cattle stealing. He found a kill-crazy gang.

Mary Allison, rancher's daughter. She started out to shoot Jim and ended up by loving him!

Crane Allison, her father. He was charged with murder. Was he guilty?

Carter Renshaw, boss of the Double-R. He was rich and handsome, but he wanted much more!

Sime Price, bank president. He offered $5,000 for *dead* robbers — not one cent for *live* ones!

Ward Grimes, saloon keeper. He collected the reward and never lived to enjoy it!

Preston Grimes, his brother. His shoulder draw was a sure sign of death!

Woll Baylor, sheriff of Lorenzo. He was smart enough to send for Jim Woodard!

1

Old Sime Price, president and chief stock-holder of the Lorenzo Bank, stumped out of the two-story false-front that housed the bank, armed with a hammer, a square of white pasteboard and a mouthful of tacks.

Price was tall, angular, though broad-shouldered, with a long, scrawny neck that rose out of a very low collar. He had a large head scantily covered with hair — a head that gave an effect of both physical and mental hardness. His sunken, smooth-shaven face seemed to bear witness that the owner was one who pushed frugality to the borders of vice.

With his congress gaiters planted solidly on the board sidewalk, Price went to work on the front of the building. He shoved the white placard into place, drove the tacks home with vicious emphasis. Then, with a grunt of satisfaction, he stepped back and grimly surveyed his handiwork.

In glaring black on white the notice
read —

REWARD
FIVE THOUSAND DOLLARS FOR
DEAD BANK ROBBERS. NOT ONE
CENT FOR LIVE ONES!

For months the whole southwest section
of the Nueces country had been plagued
with bank robberies. The bankers of the section, exasperated and alarmed, had primed
themselves for drastic action. Their final
decision, largely instigated by Price, was the
reward notice that now appeared simulta-
neously on the front of every bank building
of the section.

"There ain't no sense in ketchin' the hellions and lockin' 'em up," Price had declared. "They hire smart lawyers who rig up
perjured testimony, provide alibis and get
'em off. What happened over to Dynham?
And at Ewell? Them sidewinders were as
guilty as hell. But did they go to jail? No!
They're maverickin' around right now, and
I'll bet my last peso that some of 'em had a
hand in the Loma Alta safe crackin' and the
Laredo stage holdup last week. Don't tell
me nothin' different. The only way to put a
stop to it is to plant 'em. When I was fightin'

Injuns under General Steel, we use ta say — 'The only good Injun is a dead Injun'. Uh-huh, and the only bank robber safe outa the way is a dead one."

Some of Price's associates were dubious about going to such extremes, but the ruthless old former cattleman and Border fighter overruled the more tolerant and had his way.

Less than a week later a young cowboy walked rather unsteadily into the bank. He slouched to the cashier's cage and glared through the grating, fumbling at a pocket the while.

"What do yuh want?" the cashier asked suspiciously, staring at the puncher's flushed face.

"Money," the cowboy growled truculently. "And be quick about it." He half raised his hand to the sill of the cage.

The cashier gave a frightened yelp and ducked under his counter.

"Robbers!" he screeched. "Help! help!"

His hysterical yell brought instant results. A tall, black-coated man, who had entered the bank a moment after the cowboy, and who was now preparing to make out a deposit slip at one of the high tables, whirled around, hand streaking to his gun. There was a flash of fire, the boom of a shot.

The cowboy threw up his hands, staggered, and slumped to the floor, drilled through the back of the head. The tall man, smoking gun in hand, bounded across the room and bent over his victim, gun ready for further action. But the cowhand was already dead.

The tall man holstered his gun with swift ease, and, as the cashier came from behind the grill, he picked up something from the floor and slipped it into his pocket.

The bank was in an uproar. Old Sime Price came pounding out of his office. He took in the situation at a glance.

"Good work, Grimes!" he called to the black-coated man. "So yuh got one of the sidewinders. Who the hell is it? Know him?"

"It's young Tom Allison of the Bar A," said Grimes, peering into the cowboy's dead face. "He was playin' poker in my place a little while ago, losing."

"And figgered to make up his losses in here, eh?" growled Price. "A good chore, Ward; a mighty good chore, and one that'll be wuth money to you."

Ward Grimes, owner of the Rambler saloon, Lorenzo's biggest, smiled complacently, a gleam in his black eyes.

"I didn't think of that," he said. "I figgered it wasn't no time to take chances. He was reachin' when I throwed down on him."

"That's right," corroborated the still trembling cashier. "His hand was goin' inter his pocket when I ducked under the counter. 'I want money,' he said, and was goin' for his gun. 'Nother minute and he'd have had the drop on all of us. Wonder what old Crane Allison will have to say?"

"Never mind about Crane Allison," grunted Price. "He's allus been a trouble-maker."

The following day, Sime Price, with his board of directors and prominent stockholders sitting in solemn attendance, paid five thousand dollars to Ward Grimes, and again congratulated him on his swift sizing up of the situation. Undoubtedly, Price maintained, he had prevented a holdup of the Lorenzo bank.

Grimes modestly deprecated his feat, and accepted the five thousand. The town buzzed over the happening. Some expressed surprise that Tom Allison should have turned to robbery. For although he drank and gambled, failings not uncommon to young cowhands, he had never been mixed up in anything unlawful, so far as anybody knew. Others maintained that it was just what could be expected of the son of old Crane Allison, a salty hombre if there ever was one. Some of the more thoughtful predicted that the thing wasn't ended yet, and wondered what Crane Allison might do about it. They soon found out.

The day after young Tom Allison was buried under the whispering pines that surrounded the Bar A ranchhouse, a lanky, bleak-faced old man rode into town. He had a rifle in his saddleboot, and an old single-action Russian model Forty-four slung low against his right thigh. He dismounted, hitched his horse to a convenient rack and strode across the street to the swinging doors of Ward Grimes' saloon.

Business was good in the Rambler, though it was but early afternoon. Ward Grimes stood at the far end of the bar, smoking a cigar, a contemplative look on his swarthy face as he estimated the day's "take."

Suddenly through the babble of talk sounded a long-drawn yell.

"Ward Gri-i-i-imes!"

A dead silence fell inside the saloon. There were old-timers in the crowd, and they instantly recognized that long-drawn yell for what it was — the challenge of a gun-packin' gent inviting his enemy to come out and "talk it over" through the smoke.

The proprietor of the Rambler stiffened. The cigar fell from his suddenly limp fingers. He stared toward the swinging doors.

"Ward Gri-i-i-imes!"

Again came the yell, grim, insistent.

"It's old Crane Allison!" somebody exclaimed, peering through a window. "He's heeled!"

All eyes turned to Ward Grimes, who stood rigid at the end of the bar. How would he take it?

There was only one way he could "take" it, if he cared anything for the respect of his associates. That was to walk out of the saloon ready to accept the challenge. Otherwise he would "crawl."

A low hum ran over the room. Grimes glanced about, and met the battery of eyes trained on him. He hesitated an instant longer, then seemed to gather himself together. With queer, jerky steps he walked to the swinging doors, his knuckles whitening from the force with which he gripped his gun butt. At the doors he halted, then went through them with a rush, jerking his six from its sheath. The air exploded to a roar of gunfire.

Five seconds later, Ward Grimes lay on the board sidewalk in front of his saloon, retching and moaning, a bullet through his right shoulder, another through his left leg.

Old Crane Allison, one shirt sleeve shot to ribbons, a red smear across one sunken cheek, stood stern and erect, staring down at the prostrate killer of his son.

Fifteen minutes later, Grimes was being patched up in the doctor's office, who " 'lowed" he had a chance to pull through. Crane Allison was in jail, with a charge of attempted murder being prepared against him.

The whole section seethed with argument over the shooting. Sime Price and his banker associates staunchly upheld Ward Grimes, pointing out that a coroner's jury had absolved Grimes of blame in the killing of young Tom Allison, and denouncing old Crane Allison for taking the law into his own hands.

Crane Allison's friends, and they were many, chiefly among the cowmen, maintained that Allison had sufficient provocation for shooting it out with Grimes. He had but followed the code of the Old West, they asserted. They called to the attention of all and sundry that young Tom Allison had no record of law-breaking and had been no wilder than any number of young cowhands of the section. Price countered with the cashier's testimony that young Allison had demanded money when he approached the window, and had "reached" in the direction of his gun. The fact was stressed that he was not one of the bank's depositors. What right, then, did he have to come into the bank and demand money? He must have had robbery in mind when he did so, Price declared.

While the argument was at its height, another killing took place at nearby Dynham. A worker in one of the mines was caught loitering in an alley back of the Dynham bank in the early dusk by a newly appointed deputy town marshal, who had formerly been a bartender. The deputy started questioning him and the man, said the deputy, reached for his gun. The deputy shot him. On the dead man's person was found a half-stick of dynamite and a short length of fuse. Evidently, the deputy maintained, the man planned to blow the bank vault.

The Dynham bankers agreed with him, and another five thousand dollars in reward money was paid out.

"Good work!" declared Sime Price. "A little more of this and the section will be cleaned of the varmints."

"But it hasn't stopped bank holdups," his opponents countered when, shortly afterward, the banks at Oakville, Eagle and Casterville were robbed in quick succession and with an expert efficiency that was bewildering.

Old Sime exulted grimly, however, when two Mexicans were slain in the doorway of the Armstrong bank. They had been accosted by the town marshal, who saw them loitering there. An argument ensued. The Mexicans maintained evasively that they were waiting for a man to meet them. In the course of the argument, the marshal said, one had drawn a knife. He shot them both, and collected rewards for both.

Gaunt, uncommunicative Sheriff Woll Baylor was outspoken in his disapproval of Sime Price's reward offers. He had been an associate of Sime's in the days of their hectic youth, and the two were firm friends though often differing over matters of policy.

"You fellers are playin' the damn fool, Sime," Sheriff Baylor declared bluntly. "Yuh're payin' out good money for what? For the questionable killin's of some shiftless scum, and all the while, sidewinders with plenty of savvy are raisin' hell hereabouts and shovin' a chunk under the corner."

" 'Pears to me it's the business of the sheriff's office to put a stop to that," Price interpolated sarcastically.

"I ain't arg'fyin' *that*," Baylor admitted. "But that's beside the question. I'm talkin' about what you banker fellers are doin'. Bank robbery ain't a capital offense in Texas, so long as nobody gets hurt, but you fellers are makin' it one."

"Hellions with bank-robbin' notions had oughta be killed," the indomitable old Sime declared.

"Mebbe so," Baylor replied, "but it ain't the law of the land, and you fellers ain't no more business takin' the law inter yore own hands than anybody else. Yuh're walkin' on mighty thin ice, Sime, and sooner or later somethin' is gonna happen that won't be nice. Yuh'll end up packin' a hefty load on yore conscience."

"My conscience ain't never failed me yet," growled Price, and put to end a conversation that had already continued too long.

Another outspoken deprecator of Old Sime's program was Carter Renshaw, owner of the big Double R spread. An exceedingly tall, handsome man, clean shaven, with curling golden hair and glittering eyes, he was a comparative newcomer in the section, having arrived the year before from the Big Bend country. He had bought the Double R from Peaseley Wallace, a shiftless individual with scant ambition, a fast gun hand

17

and a liking for red-eye. Renshaw kept Wallace on as foreman of the spread, a job he was fitted for both by experience and natural ability, when sober. Renshaw kept him sober when there was work to be done. Wallace spent most of his leisure hours in Ward Grimes' Rambler saloon.

Renshaw made the ranch pay, which Wallace never had. He got rid of the few slipshod punchers that made up Wallace's outfit, and brought in his own men. They were hard-eyed, alert and efficient cowhands who did their work well and kept largely to themselves, although they could be sociable enough on occasion. Renshaw and his men became very well liked in the section.

The owner of the Double R was generally a man of even temper, but he was far from even-tempered when he rode to Sheriff Baylor's office to report the widelooping of a herd of prime beef cattle from his southwest range.

"We trailed the hellions across the Bar A and past Coffin Mountain to the desert," he said. "We lost 'em out there on that burned-over mess of shiftin' sands. Sime Price is to blame for all this hell raisin', Baylor."

"Now, now, Cart," protested the sheriff. "Yuh ain't got no right to go blamin' Sime for what's happenin'. How do yuh figger he's to blame, anyhow?"

"How do I figger it?" exploded Renshaw. "Here's how. Every owlhoot in Texas has heard about them rewards him and the other bankers are offerin'. They figger if the banks can afford such reward money, there must be fat pickin's in the section, and they're flockin' in. I tell yuh, we ain't seen nothin' yet, Baylor. You watch! Nothin's gonna be safe hereabouts from now on. What's happened is just the beginnin'. Wait till them hellions what are driftin' in learn what the Laredo stage carries. Just wait! Price is plumb loco, and you know it."

"He's stubborn as a blue-nosed mule," Baylor admitted. "Mebbe yuh're right about what yuh're sayin', Cart."

"You know damn well I'm right!" growled Renshaw. "But what about my beefs? You gonna try and run them hellions down?"

"Yuh say yuh trailed 'em to the desert," Baylor pointed out. "The county line is right down there, Cart. Yuh know I got no authority beyond that line."

With a disgusted snort, Renshaw flung out of the office and headed for the Rambler saloon.

Sheriff Baylor sat alone in his office, his brows knitted, thinking deeply. Finally he drew pen and ink from a drawer and laboriously scrawled a letter. He addressed the envelope to "Captain Mort Quigley, Cattleman's Protective Association."

2

The southwestern part of McMullen County, Texas, is quite rough, with various elevations rising — in local estimation — to the dignity of mountains. One of the most noted of these is Coffin Mountain, famous in tradition and legend. Bandits who preyed on traffic over the "lower trail" from Laredo to San Antonio holed up in Coffin Mountain, as did other gentlemen of questionable antecedents and unpredictable futures.

Coffin Mountain came rightly by its sinister name. Many a body had desiccated in the dry air on and around that ominous hill. One could have turned up dusty bones almost anywhere in the thickets that clothed its sides, or found skeletons glaring from empty sockets in the gloom of the caves that honeycombed its cliffs and ledges.

South of Coffin Mountain ran a trail from which the gray shimmer of a bay could be seen, a trail that slithered across the seventy terrible miles of parched desert to the Rio Grande. It followed the coastline for some distance, then turned sharply north to glide in the shadow of the mountain, from the main street of Lorenzo, until it finally reached San Antonio. The *Pasajero* — Traveler — Trail, it was named, probably because, according to old-timers, "gents ridin' it usually shore do travel!"

The man who rode northward along the trail, some two weeks after Sheriff Baylor wrote his letter to Mort Quigley, could hardly be called "traveling," although his magnificent red-golden sorrel had the look of a cayuse that could make speed a-plenty, should occasion arise. And the man was as noteworthy as the splendid animal he forked. Very tall, much more than six feet, he was deep of chest, broad of shoulder, lean of waist and hips. He wore the homely garb of the rangeland — overalls, soft blue shirt, vivid handkerchief looped about his sinewy throat, dimpled, broad-brimmed "J.B.," batwing chaps, and well-worn boots of softly tanned leather. Double cartridge belts encircled his waist, while from the carefully oiled and worked cut-out holsters protruded the black butts of heavy guns. His face was deeply bronzed, lean as to cheek, with a powerful jaw, a high-bridged nose with sensitive nostrils, a rather wide mouth, grin-quirked at the corners, and long, level green eyes set beneath thick black brows. He lounged in the saddle with the careless grace of a lifetime on horseback.

Both horse and rider were thickly powdered with the gray dust of the desert, though neither showed any signs of fatigue despite this evidence of long and hard journeying. Thus, beneath hurrying cloud wrack, rode Jim Woodard, ace man of the Cattleman's Association — Jim Woodard, the Range Rider.

The night showed promise of being a wild one. The angry red of the sunset had faded in the west amid a tossing mass of turbulent clouds, while from the waters of the bay came a low moaning. The naked tree branches tossed wildly in a wailing wind. A sibilant hissing and rustling ran through the mesquite. New clouds of dust rose from the surface of the trail — cosmic dancers of the night, writhing and twisting, pirouetting grotesquely.

To the north were vast reaches of wild, thorny pasture. Woodard could hear *ladino* cows popping the bushes, though not a horn was in sight.

"She's quite a section, Rojo," he told his horse. "Reckon most anything can happen hereabouts, and most generally does. Wonder how much farther we got to go to reach that darn town of Lorenzo. Sure could stand a s'roundin' of chuck about now. And I've a notion you sorta hanker to put on the nose-bag, you darn old grass burner. We swallowed so much dust crossing that infernal desert that by now we musta growed chicken gizzards to take care of it. June along, hoss, we got places to go."

The trail curved away from the moaning bay and flowed north, with a slight trend to the east. Still far ahead, the mass of Coffin Mountain shouldered the sky and its vast shadow fell across the trail and darkened the chaparral beyond. Over the craggy summit of the mountain hung a blood-red moon, now burning luridly, now obscured by the racing cloud wrack. An owl whistled eerily from the top of a blasted pine. A disgruntled coyote answered with a querulous yipping. Somewhere a steer wailed thinly. A nighthawk almost brushed Woodard's face with it's silent wings and its vicious scream set Rojo, the horse, to snorting and dancing.

"Steady," Woodard told him. "That feller is just big talk. He wouldn't tackle anything heftier than a jackrabbit. That is if he was a hawk at all, and not a ghost of Lafitte or Moro or some other of the old pirate gents who usta ride herd out there on the bay. This is just the sorta night yuh could expect them to be maverickin' around."

Rojo snorted his disgust and Woodard chuckled. He gazed toward the black mass of the mountain and Rojo's head turned north. There was something grim and menacing about the huge, inchoate bulk, with the red moon hanging over it like a sullen danger light and the thickening cloud veil dimming the stars.

Suddenly the red light of the moon seemed to reflect from the mountain top as from a mirror. Swiftly the reddish glow under the irregular red disc spread and heightened. It became a leaping flame that danced and flickered. For several moments it burned fiercely, then abruptly died and vanished.

"Now what in blazes?" wondered the Range Rider. "Why would somebody build a fire up top that pile of rocks and then douse it just as it got going good?"

He continued to stare toward the mountain top as he rode, but there was no repetition of the phenomenon. The rocky crest remained dark and shadowy, with only the glow of the moonlight seeping over its crags. Woodard shrugged his shoulders and gave his attention to his more immediate surroundings.

In the east began a low mutter of thunder,

with occasional lightning flickers. The rolling wall of cloud curved over the zenith, crept westward. The stars vanished, then the moon. The night became black as pitch.

Louder and louder sounded the thunder. The wind increased in volume. To Woodard's ears again came the lonely moan of the bay. Loosened twigs began to spatter down on the trail.

Rojo's ears suddenly pricked sharply forward. A moment later Woodard heard what had attracted the sorrel's attention. Swelling out of the north was a pounding beat.

"Horses," the Range Rider muttered. "Lots of 'em, and coming this way fast."

He pulled Rojo to a halt and sat listening intently.

"Better give those hustling gents plenty of room," he decided. He backed Rojo off the trail and into the fringe of brush. The pounding hoofbeats swelled to a rumbling roar that drowned the thunder overhead. They were directly ahead, now. A moment later and they surged past to the accompaniment of the rumbling and bleating of irritated cattle.

Suddenly the sky flamed as a jagged lightning flash split the clouds from horizon to zenith. The scene was instantly as bright as day.

In the bluish glare Woodard had a vision of tossing horns, rolling eyes and shaggy backs. The herd was almost past where he sat his horse at the edge of the trail. Riding hard on the heels of the cattle, with loose rein and busy spur, were half a dozen horsemen who urged the lumbering cows to greater efforts.

Woodard heard a startled yell from their ranks. Instantly he went sideways from the saddle.

There was a roar of gunfire, a crackling of bullets through the branches over his head. Rojo snorted explosively and lunged back into the brush. Prone on the ground, Woodard jerked both guns from their sheaths and sent a stream of lead hissing toward the unseen horsemen, who were now enveloped in the blackness of the night. A yell of pain echoed the shots. A bullet or two whined past in answer; but the roll of hoofbeats was undiminished. Swiftly they faded into the south.

"Nice little reception committee," the Range Rider muttered wrathfully as he got to his feet and dusted himself off. "Reckon we winged one of the hellions, from the way he yelped. Now what is this all about? Slinging lead at a plumb stranger! They sure were shoving those cows along. I've a prime notion some spread hereabouts is gonna be missing a herd of beefs come morning."

Again the lightning flamed in the sky, but revealed only an empty stretch of trail to the next bend. Woodard stared southward a moment, then got Rojo out of the brush, forked him and rode north. He loosened his slicker from behind the cantle and donned it, buttoning it close about his throat. A moment later came a spatter of raindrops that quickly increased to a steady downpour. Rojo's glossy coat streamed water. Woodard cuffed his hat over one eye to let the rain slosh off without obscuring his vision.

Not that there was much of anything to see. The night, except when the blue glare of the lightning beat against the veil of rain, was again as black as the inside of a bull in fly time.

Gradually, however, the rain lessened. The storm went roaring westward, booming its way across the desert. Stars appeared in the east. Then the moon, almost below the topmost crags of the mountain, sent a reddish beam drifting across the sodden growth; and in the sudden flood of bloody radiance, Woodard saw the dark bulk of a ranchhouse a little distance to the right of the trail.

"Well, this is something like it," he told his horse. "Reckon a plumb wet and hungry gent had oughta be able to drop a loop on a bed here. We'll chance it, anyhow."

A beaten roadway curved from the trail to the door of the ranchhouse. Woodard rode up it a little way, reined Rojo in and shouted. Etiquette of the rangeland forbade riding up to a door and knocking after dark, even though the hour was not particularly late.

For several minutes there was no response to his hail. Then a light flickered inside the house. Woodard saw a shadow cross a window in the direction of the door. He swung down from the saddle and mounted the veranda steps, whistling softly under his breath.

There was the rattle of a drawn bolt, the door swung open, and Woodard stiffened, his hands hovering above the black butts of his guns.

He was staring squarely into the muzzle of a leveled rifle.

But it was not the threatening muzzle that caused the Range Rider's eyes to widen with astonishment. Back of the gun was a small, red-haired, blue-eyed girl.

For a moment Woodard was at a loss what

to do or say. Then his rather wide mouth quirked at the corners, his strangely colored eyes grew sunny, and he chuckled.

"Ma'am," he drawled, "when yuh take a notion to throw down on a gent, it's a mighty good idea not to have the hammer of yore shootin' iron on safety. Yuh just nacherly couldn't get anywhere with that hammer where it is right now."

The girl gave a startled gasp. Her glance dropped to the stock of the Winchester. Woodard was right. The hammer was at half-cock.

Her glance flew back to the laughing eyes of the tall man who fronted her, and under the undisguised amusement of his gaze, she blushed hotly. Woodard was standing with the thumbs of his slender, powerful hands hooked over his cartridge belts. Directly under his palms were the black butts of his long-barreled Colts. The girl with the half-cocked Winchester in her hands was as help-less as if it had been in the next county.

Abruptly she lowered the rifle.

"Come in," she said, "and stop laughing at me!"

Woodard glanced over his shoulder.

"My horse?" he remarked.

"I'll have him taken care of right away," replied the girl. "Come in, before the wind blows the light out."

Woodard entered, closing the door behind him, and began unbuttoning his slicker, his level gaze meanwhile taking in his surroundings. As he removed the wet coat, a cautious step sounded on the porch outside. The girl turned quickly.

"An old feller with gray whiskers," Woodard remarked. "He was looking in the window just a minute ago."

"It's Stiffy, one of my hands," the girl said. She crossed to the door and opened it. "Come in, Stiffy," she called.

A blocky old fellow sidled into the room, glancing suspiciously at Woodard.

"I heerd this feller whoop," he announced. "Figgered I'd better snuk up and see who it was. Thought mebbe it might be that pesky Carter Renshaw snoopin' around."

"Now, now, Stiffy," the girl chided gently. "Mr. Renshaw has never done anything wrong. He's been very kind."

"Don't like him," grunted Stiffy. "Don't like his eyes. They're yaller, like a cat's."

"I've known some purty nice cats," Woodard interpolated with a chuckle.

"Uh-huh, they're nice — when they want somethin' of yuh," Stiffy growled. "But rub their fur the wrong way a mite and see what happens."

"Don't reckon any of us pertickler like having our fur rubbed the wrong way," Woodard replied smilingly.

Stiffy grunted. He ran his eye over the Range Rider's towering form with distinct approval.

"I'll look after yore horse," he offered. "I've a notion this feller could stand a mite of chuck and a cup or two of steamin' coffee, Miss Mary," he added. "He's damp as if he'd been ridin' the river. I'll get a fire goin' in the stove soon as I bed down that cayuse."

"Yuh got something there, feller," Woodard agreed. "But I'll get the fire going, if yuh'll show me where the kitchen is located hereabouts."

"I'll show you," said the girl. "I'm sorry about the way I greeted you, but we've had trouble in this section and never know what to expect. We're a little suspicious of strangers."

"Yuh don't appear pertickler scairt, though," Woodard remarked.

"No," the girl replied slowly, "a woman instinctively knows whom she should fear. I don't fear you, and I don't think I ever would. Nor would any woman, for that matter."

"Thank yuh, Ma'am," Woodard said.

31

"Besides, I saw Stiffy took a liking to you at first glance," the girl added. "My father always said Stiffy was a mighty good judge of people. That's why I can't understand why he's taken such a dislike to Carter Renshaw. Mr. Renshaw owns the spread over to the east of ours. He has been very kind since my father was — was taken away."

"Yuh mean yore father is dead, Ma'am?" the Ranger asked sympathetically.

The girl's soft lips tightened.

"My father is in jail," she replied quickly. "In jail for shooting the man who murdered my brother."

3

Woodard stared at the girl, after this rather startling announcement, at a loss just what to say. Before he could speak, she abruptly changed the subject.

"The kitchen is out this way," she said, taking a lamp from the table. "If you'll get the fire started, I'll make us some supper. I'm hungry, too."

In the big roomy kitchen of the ranchhouse, Woodard soon had a fire going in the range. The girl busied herself with various utensils. A few minutes later old Stiffy stumped in.

"That's some horse yuh have, son," he said to Woodard. "He's all took care of proper. I'm goin' to bed. You younkers are able to stay up and gab all night, but an old feller has to have his rest."

"We'll try and finish getting that herd together on the south range, tomorrow," the girl told him.

"Uh-huh," agreed Stiffy. "We'd ought to finish 'er up tomorrow. I'll bet the boys down there are cussin' about now. That rain was a drencher."

With a nod to the Range Rider, he left the room. Soon Woodard and the girl sat down to an appetizing meal.

"I suppose you were rather surprised at what I said back in the living room," the girl remarked. "Guess I'd better tell you about it. I'm Mary Allison. My father is Crane Allison, and this is the Bar A ranch."

Woodard supplied his name in turn, and then for some time he listened intently to the girl's account of what had recently happened in the section.

"My brother had never been in any trouble," Mary Allison concluded. "I don't say he wasn't wild and reckless. Most of the young men of this section are. But I know he would never have had anything to do with a crime like bank robbery."

"Why, do yuh suppose, did he go into the bank that way and ask for money?" Woodard asked.

"I have no idea," the girl replied. "I feel that possibly the cashier might have misunderstood what he said. The banks are jittery around here of late. There has been lots of trouble."

"He couldn't have been asking for a loan?"

The girl slowly shook her head.

"He would have known he couldn't get a loan from the bank," she replied. "You see, my brother was two years younger than I am, and I'm only past twenty-one. He was not of age and couldn't have borrowed money from the bank, having no security to offer."

"If yore father would have agreed to indorse his note, he might have been able to," Woodard pointed out.

Again the girl shook her head.

"My father would have had no security either," she explained. "You see, it is not generally known, but the ranch is in my name. My mother owned the spread when my father married her, and she willed it to me. My father was my guardian until last year, but then the property came to me."

"I see," Woodard nodded thoughtfully.

"The bankers are doing a terrible thing by

offering those rewards," the girl observed bitterly. "They are putting a premium on murder."

"Taking the law inter yore own hands is allus bad business," Woodard agreed gravely. "They are convicting folks before they are brought to trial. Doubtless, though, they feel they are justified."

"It hasn't stopped the bank robberies," the girl countered. "There have been more since the rewards were offered than before."

"Any other trouble in this section?" Woodard asked.

"A lot of cattle have been stolen."

"Where do they run 'em? Stolen cows are no good unless yuh can find a market."

"To Mexico, I suppose," the girl replied.

"Across seventy miles of desert?"

"Where else could they take them? They certainly couldn't keep them in the section, and they couldn't run them north or east. There is nothing to the west of here but hills and desert. Not a ranch within a hundred miles. They would have to take them south. There is no trailing anything across the desert between here and the Rio Grande. The sands are constantly shifting and wipe out all tracks. A big herd was run off Carter Renshaw's Double R just a couple of weeks back. Renshaw trailed them out onto the desert, and lost the trail there. They were headed southwest — toward Mexico."

Woodard said nothing further, but his black brows drew together until the concentration furrow was deep between them.

They were enjoying a final cup of steaming coffee when a clatter of hoofs sounded outside. A moment later the bunkhouse door banged open. An excited chatter of voices was followed by steps running swiftly toward the ranchhouse. The girl hurried to the door and flung it open.

Old Stiffy and another elderly waddie entered, supporting between them a younger cowboy who reeled drunkenly on dragging feet. His eyes were wild, his face white and haggard. One cheek was crusted with dried blood that had oozed from a ragged furrow just above his left eyebrow.

"Chuck!" gasped the girl. "What happened to you?"

"Plugged!" the cowboy mumbled. "Knocked me off my horse and down inter the brush. Reckon the hellions figgered I was done for. Anyhow, they didn't come to finish me. The rain brought me to. Managed to catch my horse and hang on till I got here."

"Where's Watson?" asked the girl.

"Dead," replied the cowboy. "Drilled dead

center. They got the herd."

"Who did it?" demanded Stiffy.

"How the hell would I know?" answered Chuck. "I heerd horses comin' outa the brush, then the hull world blew up inside my head. When I come to, I found Watson cashed in. The herd was gone."

As Stiffy was about to voice another question, Woodard interrupted.

"Fust chore is to look after this feller," he said. "Set him down in that chair. Get me rags and hot water. That head of his needs attention."

With swift, efficient hands he cleansed the wound. He probed the skull beneath with sensitive fingers and decided that there was no fracture.

"Hit yuh a nasty lick, but yuh'll be all right soon as the headache wears off," he told the puncher. "Yuh say yuh didn't see any of the hellions?"

The cowboy wearily shook his head.

"Didn't see nothin'," he reiterated.

"I figger *I* did, though," Woodard remarked. His hearers glanced inquiry at him. Briefly he recounted what had happened on the trail south of Coffin Mountain.

"That would be the herd, all right," Stiffy declared. "Headin' for the desert. How many of the hellions was there?"

37

"About six, I'd say," Woodard replied. "They were shovin' the cows along almighty fast. Too fast to make sense, I'd say."

"How's that?" asked Stiffy.

"As yuh know, cows can soon be run off their feet," Woodard explained. "A plumb down herd could never make it across the desert. Those hellions must have known that they didn't have anything to worry about — that there wasn't a chance of anybody being on their tail. They evidently figgered they'd done for both night hawks, and that it would be way past morning before anybody found out what had happened. Why all the hurry?"

"The owlhoot sort is allus scairt of somethin'," was Stiffy's explanation.

Woodard did not comment further.

"This feller had better be got to bed," he said as he finished bandaging the wounded puncher's head.

"And, Stiffy, you and Jasper ride out in the morning and bring in poor Watson's body," the girl directed.

After the cowboys had departed, Woodard and the girl sat regarding each other.

" 'Pears yore troubles are piling up, Ma'am," the Range Rider observed sympathetically.

"Yes," the girl answered. "The loss of those cattle hurts. I have obligations to meet. Poor Watson's death leaves me very short handed, too. Good riders are hard to get in this section."

She eyed the Range Rider contemplatively as she spoke.

"Are you just passing through?" she asked.

"That depends," Woodard replied. "If I could tie onto a good job of riding I might stick around a spell."

"I can use another tophand," the girl offered.

Woodard countered with a question. "How far is it to that town of Lorenzo, the county seat?"

"Lorenzo is twenty miles north of here, by way of the Pasajero Trail, the trail you were following," the girl replied.

"I'd figgered on riding up there tomorrow, and anyhow I reckon the sheriff's office had oughta be notified of this widelooping. If that's satisfactory to you, Ma'am, I'll be back before dark."

"That will be fine," Mary Allison replied to the oblique acceptance of the job she offered.

"Then I reckon I'll pound my ear for a spell," Woodard said. "Been up for quite a while."

"You can sleep in the spare room, just off the living room," the girl replied. "You'll find it comfortable. Stiffy used to sleep there, but he says he'd rather be in the bunkhouse, where he can listen to the boys talk in their sleep. He says he's got the whole outfit paying hush money to him."

For the first time since meeting her, Woodard saw her smile.

"I've a notion she's one mighty purty girl when she's happy," he told himself a little later, as he sat on the comfortable bed in the spare room, cleaning and oiling his guns. "Not that she's hard to look at as it is," he added.

As is often the way with men who ride much alone, Woodard had a habit of talking to his horse, or even his guns. Now he held converse with the big Colts as he gave them a careful going over.

"Looks like I'm getting a break," he told them. "This job of riding will give me an excuse for hanging around in the section, and I got a hunch that whatever happens hereabouts is going to sorta center on this spread. The old man in jail, the boy killed. A trouble-building situation for fair. And from what that old sheriff wrote Captain Mort, it looks like plenty is bustin' loose. Wonder what about that killing? Sure doesn't look as if a girl like her could have a brother who'd go in for bank robbing, but

40

yuh never can tell. It's sure for certain the old man is a salty proposition. Shot it out with the jigger who downed his son, in reg'lar Old West style. I'll hafta try and get a word with him. Wonder where in blazes these widelooped steers get to? It's just about sure they aren't run across the desert to *mañana* land. But if they aren't, as the girl 'lowed, where do they take them? After looking the section over a mite, I may be able to find an answer to that."

Woodard was in the saddle early the following morning. He found Lorenzo to be a typical cowtown with the appearances of being plenty lively on occasion. In front of a squat building with barred windows he dismounted and left Rojo tied securely. "Sheriff's Office" read a battered sign swinging above the door.

Mounting a couple of steps, he shoved open the door and entered. A lanky old fellow sitting at a table cleaning a gun looked up and nodded a greeting.

"You the sheriff?" Woodard asked.

The oldster shook his head. "Nope," he replied, "sheriff's out right now. I'm in jail here."

Woodard glanced at the wide open door leading to the cells in the back of the building, and surveyed the comfortably furnished office.

"Sorta nice jail," he commented.

"Fair to middlin'," the other agreed. "Sorta drafty of nights, when Woll Baylor fergits and leaves that door open. Woll is the sheriff. He's all right, only he's got a bad habit of wakin' me up at all hours to tell me his troubles. Reckon he's got plenty, all right. Last night he was wonderin' if he couldn't arrange it to stay here in jail for a spell and let me be sheriff."

"Mebbe he's got something there," Woodard smiled.

"Mebbe," the other nodded, "but I couldn't see it. Pull up a chair and save boot leather."

Woodard accepted the invitation and sat down. He fished out the makin's and rolled a cigarette with the slim fingers of his left hand.

"Reckon yuh're Crane Allison," he remarked.

" 'Low to be," the oldster admitted. "How come yuh to know me, son?"

"I'm working for yuh," Woodard replied. "Anyhow, yore daughter hired me to a job of riding last night."

Crane Allison gave him a sharp look.

"That so?" he said. "How's things down

to the spread?"

"Not so good," Woodard answered. "Yuh lost a herd of cows last night, and one of yore hands, feller named Watson, was cashed in."

Crane Allison straightened in his chair.

"Watson! Hank Watson!" he exclaimed. "Are yuh shore?"

"That's what was said," Woodard replied. "Feller they called Chuck rode in with a creased head and reported it."

Allison stared at the Range Rider. "Pore old Hank," he muttered. "Pore old Hank. He'd rid for me for years."

Abruptly he got to his feet and began striding up and down the office.

"I gotta get outa this damn jail," he growled.

"Can't yuh raise bail?" Woodard asked.

"Held without bail, pendin' the outcome of that damn Ward Grimes' injuries," replied Allison. "Grimes is the feller I shot."

"Grimes in a bad way?"

"Hell, no," snorted Allison. "He's gettin' along fine. But old Sime Price, the bank president, and his outfit, have a lot of pull with the co'hts. He talked Judge Wheeler inter refusin' me bail. That's about the size of it."

The Range Rider nodded thoughtfully.

"Why are they so anxious to keep yuh locked up?" he asked.

"Just contrary cussedness, I reckon," replied Allison. "Price is stubborn as a blue-nosed mule and when he figgers he's right about somethin', all hell can't move him. Don't get me wrong, son, I'm not accusin' Sime Price of doin' anythin' underhanded. I've knowed him for years, and a more honest hellion don't live. If yuh can show him he's wrong about somethin', he'll come right out and admit it, no matter how much it hurts; but once he figgers he's right, it takes a heap of showin' to change him. He's plumb certain my boy went inter that bank to hold it up. I figger he's just as certain in his own mind that it's dangerous to have me runnin' loose, so he's doin' everythin' he can to keep me hawgtied. He's standin' up for Ward Grimes not because he has any pertickler use for Grimes, but because he figgers Grimes was justified in what he did."

Woodard nodded again. He was familiar with the type.

A silence ensued, which was finally broken by the sound of hurried steps approaching the office. A moment later the door was flung open and a tall, broad-shouldered and finely formed man hurried in. He had tawny hair inclined to curl and his eyes were a very

44

light brown. His face showed agitation.

"Hello, Renshaw," greeted Allison. "What's all the hurry?"

"I got bad news for yuh, Allison," said Renshaw, darting a keen glance at Woodard. "Where's Baylor?"

"He's out right now; expect him back any minute," replied Allison. "What's the bad news?"

"Ward Grimes is dead!"

"Dead! Why I heerd he was comin' along fine!"

"That's what everybody thought. I was over to Doc's place last night and he was chipper as a jaybird. This mornin' when Doc stepped in to look him over, he was cashed in. Doc said a blood clot musta got to his heart. A thrombosis I think he called it."

Crane Allison sat down heavily in the chair behind the table. His face was suddenly very lined and old.

"Reckon this means a murder charge agin me," he said dully.

"Mebbe the coroner's jury will hold it death by nacherel causes," comforted Carter Renshaw.

"Not with Sime Price havin' the runnin' of things hereabouts," returned Allison.

"He'll see to it a murder charge is brought in."

A moment later the door opened and lean old Sheriff Baylor entered the room.

"Just heerd the bad news, Crane," he said to Allison. "That hellion *would* hafta go and cash in. Betcha he did it outa pure spite."

"Wouldn't put it past him," agreed Allison. "Well, this cowboy feller here has somethin' to tell yuh. This is Sheriff Baylor, son. Don't believe I caught yore handle."

Woodard supplied his name, but did not identify himself further. The sheriff shook hands. Allison also introduced Renshaw. Both listened to Woodard's accounts of the happenings of the night before.

"The same bunch that run off my cows, I betcha," Renshaw declared. "Yuh didn't get a look at none of 'em, Woodard?"

"Just a blur of faces by the lightning flash," the Range Rider replied. "Wasn't paying much attention to faces, anyhow. I saw them go for their guns and was too busy getting outa line to notice anything else much. There were about six of them, I'd say."

"That's about the number we figgered to be in the bunch we trailed," commented Renshaw. "Uh-huh, it was the same bunch, yuh can lay to that. I'm goin' over to the

46

Rambler for a drink. If yuh learn anything', Woll, let me know."

He left the room and crossed the street to the saloon. Woodard, watching his progress through the window, looked suddenly thoughtful, and his black brows drew together slightly.

"Keep an eye on things here, Crane," the sheriff said to Allison. "I think I'll run up to Doc White's office and have a look at Grimes. Mebbe Doc can tell me somethin'."

Woodard got to his feet.

"Mind if I go along, Sheriff?" he asked. "I sorta wrenched my left wrist last night when I went outa the hull. Would like to have the Doc put a bandage on it."

The sheriff nodded agreement and the two left the office together.

"See me before yuh head back for the spread, son," old Crane called after them.

Doc White was a typical frontier doctor of the old school. After meeting Woodard and exchanging a few words with Baylor, he ushered them into the little inner room he used for emergency cases.

Ward Grimes' body lay on the bed, the face uncovered. His dead features were distorted, his glazed eyes bulging.

"Looks like he was hit mighty sudden and sorta choked to death," the sheriff commented.

"That's the way a thrombosis would act," replied the doctor. "His heart would be about the same as if it were suddenly paralyzed."

Woodard and the sheriff approached the bed for a closer look at the dead man. As he leaned near, the Range Rider's sensitive nostrils quivered slightly. He drew a quick breath, leaned still nearer, and stared intently into the dead man's face. Abruptly he straightened up and shot a swift, all-embracing glance around the room. But he said nothing.

A little later, as Doc White was putting a tight bandage about his sinewy left wrist, he asked a rather peculiar question.

"Any place in town a feller could buy some fruit — peaches, say?"

"Yuh couldn't buy a peach in this town at this time of the year for love or money," Doc White grunted. "Reckon yuh could get some apples over to the grocery store."

4

While Sheriff Baylor and the doctor were discussing the disposal of Ward Grimes' body, Carter Renshaw entered.

"I forgot to mention it, Doc," he said, "but

48

Grimes has a brother living in Austin. I have his address. S'pose I'd better notify him, hadn't I?"

"That's right, Cart," agreed the sheriff. "You 'tend to it, will yuh? We'll hang onto Ward's body until we get word from the brother."

Renshaw nodded and hurried out.

"I was wonderin' about Ward's place, the Rambler," remarked the sheriff. "It's a valuable property."

"S'pose the brother will take over, or dispose of it," said Doc White. "Marshal of the Last Chance would buy it, I have a notion."

Woodard had a word with Crane Allison before riding back to the Bar A ranchhouse. The old man seemed very moody and depressed.

"I do feel sorta better though, knowin' that you will be lookin' after things, son," he confessed. "Yuh got a look about yuh of bein' able to handle anythin' that might come up."

Upon arriving at the ranchhouse, Woodard had the unpleasant chore of telling Mary Allison what had occurred. The red-headed girl sat gazing straight in front of her.

"Poor Daddy," she said at length. "I'm afraid this will mean more trouble for him."

Woodard smiled down at her from his great height.

"Ma'am," he said, "I don't figger yore Dad has a thing to worry about."

Mary Allison glanced up quickly.

"What makes you say that?" she asked.

"I'm not ready to talk about it — yet," Woodard told her. "But yuh can take my word for it."

The girl gazed at his sternly handsome face.

"Do you always make people believe what you say?" she asked. "I can't imagine why you said that, but somehow I believe you have good reasons."

"I have," Woodard said briefly. "Now s'pose yuh tell me a little about the spread and the things that need to be done."

"We'll ride over it tomorrow, together," the girl said. "What needs to be done most at present is get a shipping herd together. I have a note to meet the first of the month."

"Who holds the note?" Woodard asked.

"The Lorenzo Bank. Last year Dad was of the opinion that the spread needed restocking. There was a bad drought here the year before. So we borrowed money to buy a big herd. I think he was right, but then, of course, we didn't expect the trouble that came to us since. My father is a good cow-

50

man, and so was my brother, and they ran the ranch well. Now, with both of them gone, things aren't so good. My riders are loyal to me and do the best they can, but they were always used to having my father make decisions and direct all operations. None of them seems able to take hold, and while they are fond of me, I sense that they distrust a woman boss."

"Most riders do," Woodard agreed. "I've a notion things will change from now on," he promised.

The girl gave him another steady glance.

"Yes," she said, "I've a notion they will."

Before the following day's ride was over, Woodard decided that the Bar A was a good spread but a hard one to work. A large portion of it was heavily grown with dagger, prickly pear and other similar chaparral. The whole west range, which shouldered against the hills, including grim Coffin Mountain, was a labyrinth of gorges and canyons.

"Fine places for cows to hole up in bad weather," he commented. "But an almighty tough chore to get them out. Plenty of prickly pear, I see. A desert country cow can chew enough water outa that to get by in dry spells. And the grass is good. Is there water in those canyons?"

51

"Yes, in most of them," the girl replied. "This is the best watered spead in the section."

They were riding in a southerly direction, and soon afterward they passed Coffin Mountain. Woodard glanced up the craggy sides of the elevation.

"Folks ever camp out up there?" he asked.

The girl laughed.

"I don't see why in the world anybody would," she said. "It's all rocks and thorny brush, with plenty of snakes and no water. Old-timers say that robber bands used to hide in the caves."

Woodard nodded thoughtfully, still eyeing the crags and ledges. Then with a shrug of his broad shoulders, he turned his gaze south. Some time later, from where they sat their horses on the crest of a rise, they could glimpse, some three miles farther on, the shimmer of the tossing waters of the bay, coldly gray under a cloudy sky. The expanse before them to the water's edge was drearily flat, utterly devoid of growth save for a sparse straggle of *sacaguista* grass. From the ragged escarpment on the west to the shadowy, rounded hills dimly seen in the east stretched the level monotony.

"This is the utterly worthless portion of our ranch," remarked the girl. "Isn't it strange that nothing will grow here except that salt grass? There's not a bush or a tree to be found anywhere."

Jim Woodard, who, before the murder of his father by wideloopers sent him into the Cattleman's Association, had had three years of training in a famous college of engineering, looked over the forbidding terrain with the eye of a geologist.

"Not so strange," he replied. "This whole section was once under the sea. The land is impregnated with salt, so much that nothing will grow in it. The sea retreated many, many years ago, and during the ages that have passed, a film of eroded top soil has built up to a depth sufficient to nourish the grass. But the covering of fertile soil is so thin that nothing else can find root in it. Trees or shrubs driving their roots farther down come in contact with the salt impregnated earth and can't live."

"So that's the reason," said the girl. "I suppose this section of the spread will always be worthless, then."

"Oh, it'll be all right after a while," smiled Woodard. "A million or so years from now the chances are it'll be fine. That is, if the sea doesn't take a notion to come back up here some time to reclaim it.

"Yuh never can tell, though," he added.

"Sometimes things that appear plumb wuthless are mighty valuable. I've a notion the fust folks to see the salt flats and lakes up north of El Paso figgered them to be a mighty wuthless section; but the time came when a fust-class little war was fought for control of them. And the Mexicans have been packing salt from there down inter *mañana* land for a long time, and making plenty of money outa it. No, yuh never can tell. Yuh say yuh own all this section down here? None of it belongs to the Double R?"

"No, the Double R holding doesn't extend this far south," Mary Allison replied. "Our spread is roughly in the shape of an L. We run north almost to Lorenzo, and include a width of about twelve miles between the Double R and the hills to the west. Or, rather, through the hills. They are part of our holdings. From here to the bay, the whole coastwise strip, about three miles in width, clear to the hills on the east, is part of the Bar A. The ranch was originally an old Spanish grant, you see. My grandfather, on my mother's side, obtained it from the Mexican owners, the Alvarez family, who also own much land in Mexico."

"Yore title is sound? There's been questions raised about those Spanish grants, you know."

"It was upheld by the courts, in my grandfather's time," the girl replied. "We have nothing to worry about on that score, or so I think." Then she added, a trifle grimly: "But if things don't get any better, the Lorenzo bank will have to do the worrying, if any, about the title. A few more happenings like last night's and the bank will be in the cattle business."

"I've a notion things will work out," Woodard said cheerfully. "They're allus at their wust just before they get better."

"I hope you're right," Mary Allison replied. "They certainly have been bad enough of late."

The following day, the Bar A outfit got busy assembling a shipping herd to replace the one stolen the night of Woodard's arrival in the section. Woodard found the Bar A riders were all men advanced in years. They were efficient, within their physical limitations, thoroughly conversant with the various ramifications of the cow business, but slow at their work, and decidedly old-fashioned in their notions.

And the spread was, as he had suspected, a hard one to work. The cows were largely *ladinos,* wild and rangy, and difficult to fog out of their hole-ups in the brush and in the canyons. Old Stiffy " 'lowed they come

55

right up outa the Gulf of Mexico. That's what makes 'em so dad-burned salty!"

They were fat and sleek, however, in prime condition and with plenty of meat on their bones — the kind of beef buyers are glad to get. Woodard was surprised at their excellence.

"The Old Man did a prime job of stockin' last year and the year before," Stiffy explained. "He brought in the best stuff he could buy. He 'lowed the day of the old maverickin' long horn was about done, that this section would hafta have a better breed of stock if it was goin' to compete with others in the open market. 'Low he was right about that; but he put the outfit bad in debt to do it. Him and Sime Price were on good terms, then, and he didn't have no trouble gettin' the money, and I reckon Price woulda been easy on him if things didn't break just right for a spell, knowin' the Old Man's rep'tation as a square shooter. But with Price plumb on the prod against the outfit, things is different. I 'low he ain't gonna grant no extensions. Yeah, Miss Mary needs the money this herd will bring mighty bad."

Woodard nodded thoughtfully, and redoubled his efforts to get a prime herd together.

Two days later, unexpected help came to the Bar A. Just as breakfast was over, a rotund, walrus-mustached individual rode up at the head of a dozen efficient looking young hands.

"It's Slim Dryden of the Lazy D and his men," Mary Allison exclaimed in surprise, as the cavalcade unforked before the ranch-house. "The Lazy D is to the northwest of us. Their southeast corner touches our holdings. What in the world can Slim want so early in the morning?"

The question was answered shortly by the fat, jolly owner of the Lazy D.

"Howdy, everybody?" he bellowed as he entered. "Understand yuh're gettin' a herd together, Mary. I finished my big roundup yesterday evenin'. Got my shippin' herd all bedded down up on the southeast range and ready to start to the railroad tomorrow mawnin'. Me and the boys were at sorta loose ends and figgered we might as well ride down here and lend yuh a hand."

Slim Dryden had a voice that seemed to come out of the caverns of the earth. But he also had a firm hand-clasp and an infectious grin that split his rubicund countenance from ear to ear. He shook hands with Woodard, slapped old Stiffy on the back with a force that sent him into a fit of coughing and roared for coffee. Ten minutes later he and his men went tearing down the trail in a fog of dust, headed for the south range, the most difficult to work.

"Seems to be a nice little feller," Woodard commented.

"Uh-huh," Stiffy replied dryly. "Mighty nice little feller. He's got ten notches on the handle of his gun. Looks fat and soft, but I've seed him jump three feet off the floor, standin' flat-footed and kick a jigger in the jaw, and hit him with both hands before he had time to fall. Uh-huh, Slim Dryden's a plumb nice little feller."

"He's always doing things for people," Mary Allison said, "and doing them in a way that makes it seem it's the greatest fun in the world to do them."

"I've a notion it is, for him," Woodard said.

Dryden and his hands were back just before sundown, chipper as a treeful of red-birds, and giving the general appearance of having just returned from a picnic rather than from a long day of the hardest kind of work.

"You jiggers head for our ranchhouse and get some shuteye," Dryden told his men. "We want to start shovin' that herd to the railroad tomorrow. Get the wagon started by daylight and then ride down to meet us.

I'm gonna have supper here and then spend the night with the boys in that canyon mouth. We'll start the cows movin' as soon as it's light and pick you fellers up on the trail. We won't wait to eat fust. Tell the cook to have us some chuck ready when we catch up with the wagon. Okay, get goin'."

After consuming an enormous meal, washed down with numerous cups of coffee, Dryden lighted a cigarette and rose to go.

"Gotta be headin' up for the herd," he announced. "We'll drop around again in a coupla days, Mary. Figger yuh'd oughta be about ready to shove yore cows along by then."

Jim Woddard also got to his feet.

"Figger I'll ride along with yuh a piece, if yuh don't mind," he said. "Would sorta like to get a look at the country up that way."

"Fine!" applauded the owner of the Lazy D. "We can make it before dark, if we hustle."

Dryden chattered gaily as they rode, regaling Woodard with accounts of the recent happenings in the section.

"Don't know what the country's comin' to," he complained. "Usta be plumb peaceful hereabouts, and now things are happenin' so fast yuh can't keep track of 'em.

59

Seem's Sime Price sorta pulled a trigger and set 'em off when he began offerin' them rewards. Of co'hse there'd been some bank robberies before that — been havin' 'em all over Texas, I understand. But business didn't really pick up till right after pore Tom Allison got cashed in."

The sun was behind the western crags and the sky was flaming scarlet and gold when they turned from the trail and slanted diagonally toward the hills.

"Another five minutes and we'll be there," said Dryden.

They passed through a couple of groves, rounded a shoulder of rock and the canyon mouth in question lay before them. It was narrow and dark. The sides, more than a hundred feet in height, shot straight up from the ground. The small stream that Dryden said foamed from a crack in the end wall, flowed out of the gorge and turned to the right.

Dryden gestured to the big herd bunched contentedly just inside the canyon mouth.

"Ain't she a beaut?" he said. "I ain't takin' no chances with them beefs. That's why I held 'em here in this hole instead of farther nawth. It's a plumb nacherel corral. Nobody could come at 'em except from the front, and they'd hafta ride around in back of 'em before they could start 'em movin', and I reckon me and the boys would have somethin' to say to them blasted coyotes about that."

"Suppose somebody was holed up in the canyon?" Woodard suggested.

"Hell, nobody could get in there," Dryden scoffed. "The canyon is a box and the sides and end wall are straight-up-and-down. A lizard would get dizzy tryin' to come down them rocks. The herd has been here all day and anybody what wanted to get in would hafta pass the boys. I've had four of my best hands in charge here since daylight. Nope, there's nothin' to worry about on that score."

A few minutes later they dismounted where the punchers had made their camp. Woodard was introduced and shook hands all around. One of the hands began heating up some coffee.

Woodard and Dryden stood on the stream bank and talked, the former gazing thoughtfully into the south, toward where the grim bulk of Coffin Mountain shouldered against the sky. He turned to speculate on the site of the camp, which was on a grassy flat in the canyon mouth. He glanced up the dark gorges. Then suddenly his attention became fixed on the surface of the little stream that purled at their feet. A moment later he turned to the ranch owner.

"Dryden," he said, "that's a mighty bad place to make camp. Suppose something happened to set those cows off. They'd hightail right in this direction and the camp would be right in their path."

"I put it here to keep 'em from strayin' outa the canyon," Dryden replied. "They won't come past the fire. Nothin' to worry about on a night like this. Plumb still and quiet. If it was stormy it would be somethin' else again."

"Just the same," Woodard said, "I figger yuh'd better move it up onto that ledge under the cliff, seeing as I aim to spend the night with yuh."

"Yuh're loco —" Dryden began. He glanced up at the Range Rider, who let the full force of his level green eyes rest on the other's face.

"I figger yuh'd better move it," Woodard repeated quietly.

Dryden stared at him. Then he shook his head in a bewildered fashion.

"Woodard," he complained querulously, "yuh're a almighty funny jigger. A minute ago I'd have swore I wouldn't move that camp, but somehow or other yuh've got me feelin' I'd oughta do as yuh say. Yuh got any reason for figgerin' it had oughta be moved?"

"Yes," Woodard replied briefly, "I have."

Dryden started to speak, apparently thought better of it, and snorted instead.

"Okay," he grumbled, "we'll move it, but I bet before mornin' youh'll wish yuh were sleepin' down here on this soft grass instead of up on them hard rocks. I can stand it if you can — I got more cushionin' on my bones than you have on yores."

The Lazy D punchers also grumbled, but they were evidently not in the habit of questioning the orders of their fat boss.

"What about the fire — shall we put it out?" one asked.

"Leave it alone," Woodard said. "It'll be quite a spell before it burns down," he added cryptically.

They drank their coffee beside the fire, then scrambled up through the deepening darkness to the rocky bench under the cliff. The horses were rope-corralled beside a thicket just to the right of the canyon mouth.

The cowboys and Dryden spread their blankets on the softer spots of the rock and were soon fast asleep.

Woodard also spread a blanket and lay down, but not to sleep. Half reclining

63

against a convenient boulder, he gazed over the rangeland to the south of the canyon, thinking deeply, and very much awake.

Several hours passed. The great clock in the sky wheeled westward. The stars burned golden with no film of cloud to dim their lustre.

The night was very still, with only the occasional contented rumbling of the cattle to break the silence. Woodard began to grow drowsy. Suddenly, however, his eyes opened wide.

Far to the south and high in the sky, a winking light had suddenly sprung into being. It glowed and swelled, flickered brightly for a few moments, then abruptly died to a glow and vanished.

"Now what in blazes?" muttered the Range Rider, very much awake. "It was on top that darn mountain down there, I'll bet a peso. Just the same as the one I saw the night I rode inter this section."

He continued to stare into the south for some time, but there was no repetition of the strange light in the sky. He turned over onto his side and gazed into the blackness of the canyon to rest his strained eyes.

For fully another hour he lay quiet, listening to the heavy breathing of his companions.

A sound came through the stillness, a sharp, metallic clashing that brought Woodard bolt upright on his blanket. It was such a sound as is made by a horse's iron striking a stone. It seemed to come from the blackness of the canyon.

Woodard sat listening intently, every nerve strung tight. The sound was not repeated. Then with paralyzing suddenness all hell broke loose in the black canyon. There was a roar of gunfire, a wild yelling, the snap and crackle of swung slickers, a drumroll of beating hoofs. Woodard bounded to his feet.

The cattle were milling wildly and bellowing with fright. As the pandemonium behind them continued they fled madly down the canyon, their hoofs clashing on the stones, their terrified bawls adding to the turmoil.

Tense, alert, Woodard watched the herd thunder past. Close on the heels of the panic-stricken cattle came shadowy horsemen, yelling and shooting. Woodard's hands streaked down and up. Both guns let loose with a rattling crash.

The exultant yells of the rustlers changed to howls of surprise and alarm. There was a scream of pain that ended in a choking rattle. A man pitched headlong from his saddle. An instant later another fell like a sack of old clothes.

Slim Dryden was out of his blankets, roaring profanity. He instantly sized up the situation and began shooting. The Lazy D punchers, dazed and half awake, instinctively followed suit.

The demoralized wide loopers bulged out of the canyon mouth and, bending low in their saddles, sent their frantic horses skalleyhooting through the scattering cattle at top speed. In a moment they were fading into the distance and going like the wind. Woodard sent his remaining shots whining after them. Then he began ejecting the spent shells from his guns and replacing them with fresh cartridges.

"S'pose somebody gets a fire going and some coffee heating," he remarked to his chattering companions. "I've a notion there won't be much more sleeping hereabouts tonight."

"Uh-huh, and build it up here on the bench," said Slim Dryden, adding significantly, "The one we had is tromped flat, along with everythin' else down on that grass flat!"

5

As soon as the fire was going well, they dragged the bodies of the slain rustlers into the circle of its light.

"Mean lookin' hellions, ain't they?" said Slim Dryden, bending over to peer into the contorted features. "The little one looks like he might have Injun blood."

"Ever see either of them before?" Woodard asked.

Dryden and the hands shook their heads.

One of the dead men was small and dark, with straight black hair and glazing black eyes. His companion was lanky, a little above middle height, and had straw colored hair and a straggling sandy mustache. Both wore ordinary range costume with nothing distinguishing about it.

"Scrub herd Border scum," grunted Slim Dryden.

Woodard began turning out the pockets of the dead men. He uncovered a miscellany of odds and ends of little interest.

"What's that?" Dryden asked as the Ranger drew a round tin box from the taller rustler's pocket.

Woodard turned the box over curiously in his slim fingers.

"Snuff," he said. "A box of snuff. Some jiggers use it in place of eating tobacco."

"So I've heard," admitted Dryden, "but I never knowed a cowhand to."

Woodard nodded, but did not comment.

"Their horses had oughta be around somewhere," said Dryden. "Mebbe there'll be a brand on them to tie these hellions up with somebody."

"Not likely," Woodard disagreed. "Chances are they'll wear some loco Mexican brand or none at all."

Dryden nodded. "Woodard," he said suddenly, "how come yuh to figger somebody might be up in that canyon?"

Woodard smiled down at him.

"Remember we were standing on the crick bank," he replied. "Well, I was looking down inter the crick and I saw something come floating along on top of the water. It was a cigarette butt. None of the boys were on the crick bank higher up at the time. So I figgered that butt musta come down the crick outa the canyon. It couldn't have come far, either. Otherwise the paper woulda soaked off and it would have sank. I figgered the only way it could have gotten inter the water was by some careless gent up there a little ways flipping it inter the crick after he'd finished his smoke. Right then was when I decided the flat was no place for a camp."

Dryden shook his head in admiration.

"Them eyes of yores don't miss anythin', do they!" he said. "Well, feller, I reckon we owe yuh plenty. If it hadn't been for you,

68

right now me and the boys wouldn't be any-thin' much but grease spots. I'm not the man to fergit, feller."

"Dryden, yuh went outa yore way to lend somebody a helping hand yesterday," Wood-ard replied. "Sometimes doing things like that brings unexpected and unlooked for pay."

Slim Dryden tugged his mustache and was silent.

"Them hellions musta been holed up in that gulch all day yesterday," he observed a little later. "What's got me guessin', though, is how they knew we were goin' to corral that herd in this canyon last night. I shore didn't advertise it around."

"Have any visitors to yore spread of late?" Woodard asked.

"Only fellers I know well," Dryden replied. "Night before last, old man Stevens, Sid Blake, John Bradley, Carter Renshaw and Lester James were at the ranchhouse for a settin' of poker."

"Mebbe one of them fellers stopped off at town for a drink and let a word drop that somebody overheard," suggested one of the cowboys.

"I reckon that was it," Dryden agreed. Jim Woodard looked thoughtful, but did not say anything.

Long before the scattered herd was got together again, the rest of the Lazy D outfit came up, apprehensive and concerned. Their comments anent the night's happenings were vivid and profane. Admiring and approving glances were cast at Woodard.

"Why'd yuh hafta go and let Mary Allison hire this feller ahead of yuh, Boss?" one demanded in injured tones.

"I've a notion Mary needs him wuss than I do," grunted Dryden. "I figger she's a good boss to work for, too."

"She's a heap easier on the eyes, anyhow," commented one of the older hands. "Slim shore ain't gettin' any purtier as the years roll by."

"If I looked like you, yuh dried up scantlin', I'd go drown myself in a mudhole!" bawled the indignant Dryden, amid the chuckles of his men.

After the herd got on its belated way to the railroad, Woodard headed back for the Bar A. As he rode south he often gazed at the great blocky mass of Coffin Mountain looming against the sky.

"I've a notion that darn pile of rocks holds the key to all the hell raising that's going on in this section," he mused. "But I still can't figger why somebody keeps lighting fires on top of it, and putting 'em out again before

70

they get going good."

Several busy days followed on the Bar A. The shipping herd was almost ready to take the trail when Woodard rode to town with Mary Allison to visit her father. While the girl was at the sheriff's office, Woodard dropped into the Rambler for a drink and to look the place over.

Although the hour was early, the big room was fairly well filled with a typical cow town crowd. Woodard noted a quiet-looking, sinewy man of slightly above middle height standing at the far end of the bar and apparently in charge of the establishment. He had hard black eyes, a thin-lipped mouth and sallow face.

"That's Preston Grimes, the new boss," the bartender who served Woodard remarked, noting the direction of his gaze. "Doesn't seem to be a bad feller. Not much of a talker. Different from his brother, Ward, that way. Ward was allus gabbin' about somethin'. He showed up day before yesterday and took charge. Had papers and letters from a bank over in Louisiana to prove he was Ward's only brother. Judge Hale 'lowed he might as well take charge, seein' as there was nobody to run the place. I figger the co'ht will turn the property over to him, all right."

As Woodard was sipping his drink, Carter Renshaw entered accompanied by a beefy, red-faced man with a truculent eye. They did not pause at the bar but passed to a table where some cattlemen were playing poker.

"That's Carter Renshaw who just come in," observed the sociable drink juggler. "The feller with him is his foreman, Peaseley Wallace, who usta own the Double R. Renshaw bought it from him. Cart is one of the up-and-comin' cowmen of the section. Figger he ain't gonna get on with the new boss like he did with his brother, though. They had a sorta run-in yesterday. Ward Grimes allus had a bottle of special stuff put away for Cart. Yesterday when Cart come in he asked for it. But the new boss told him he figgered to treat all his customers alike. Cart began to swell up, but Grimes just looked at him and Cart kinda pulled in his horns. He ain't the sort to take water, either."

Woodard was something of the same opinion and regarded the quiet Preston Grimes with heightened interest. He noticed that Renshaw ignored the saloonkeeper when he came in; Wallace, however, bent a hostile stare in his direction.

"I've a notion that red-faced gent is good

at getting his bristles up when he's had a snort or two," Woodard told himself.

Woodard's surmise was strengthened by Wallace's conduct in the poker game. He was evidently losing, and just as evidently couldn't take it. His grumbling voice rose higher and higher. Also, he drank constantly and his red face grew more flushed from his frequent potations.

There was a house dealer at the table, a quiet, elderly man with a soft, courteous voice. Once Woodard heard him remonstrate politely with Wallace. He got an oath and a black scowl in reply.

Suddenly the matter seemed to come to a head. Wallace threw down his cards, cursed loudly and surged to his feet. Carter Renshaw spoke restrainingly to him, but Wallace paid him no mind. He shook his left fist in the dealer's face. His right hand dropped to his gun butt. The dealer sat perfectly still with his hands spread out on the table. It was Preston Grimes who acted.

The new owner of the Rambler went across the floor like a wind-blown wraith, silently, smoothly, apparently without haste. His slim left hand, the fingers of which, Woodard noted, were waxen and tapering, gripped Wallace on the shoulder and swung him around with effortless ease. The same

73

slim left hand flickered back to its owner's left coat lapel.

With a roar, Wallace jerked his Colt. Then he froze, the barrel still pointing toward the floor. He was staring into the black muzzle of the short-barrelled gun Grimes had flickered from the shoulder holster under his left armpit. Grimes spoke, his voice flat and emotionless.

"Sit down! If you can't carry your likker any better than that, you won't get any more in here."

For a moment Wallace glared into the saloonkeeper's unwinking black eyes. Then he mumbled something under his breath, shoved his gun back into its sheath and slumped onto his chair. Grimes holstered his own weapon with effortless ease, turned on his heel and walked back to the bar.

"Salty, all right," Woodard murmured, "and lightning fast. That iron just 'growed' in his hand. Wallace wouldn't have had a chance, no matter how hard he tried."

The incident appeared to have sobered the Double R foreman. His manner became more subdued and though he scowled blackly and mumbled to himself from time to time, he no longer raised his voice. Renshaw said something to him in reproving tones, but otherwise did not appear particularly concerned with the happening. The other players seemed amused, and rather pleased.

A little later a Mexican in range costume entered the saloon, glanced about and made for Renshaw's table. He spoke to the ranch owner in Spanish. Renshaw replied in the same language. The Mexican nodded, and left the saloon.

"Felipe just came back from the railroad," Renshaw explained to his companions. "He told me we can't get cars placed for our shipping herd until Friday. Reckon we won't start that herd on the trail tomorrow, after all. Reckon we'd better head back to the spread and line up the boys, Pease. Cash in and let's go."

The pair disposed of their chips and left the saloon together. Jim Woodard thoughtfully watched them depart, the concentration furrow deep between his black brows. A few minutes later he paid for his drinks, nodded to the sociable barkeep and also departed.

The sky was heavily overcast when Woodard stepped from the saloon. By the time he reached the sheriff's office, the first drops of a brisk shower were spattering the dust of the street.

"It won't last, though," he told Mary Allison, as he gazed through the streaming window panes. "The sky is getting light in the west already. We can head back for the spread in half an hour, if yuh're ready."

Crane Allison told Woodard that a murder charge had been filed against him and that he was held without bail pending grand jury action.

"Don't let it worry yuh," the Range Rider counselled. "Just sit tight and take it easy. We'll keep things moving out to the spread till yuh get back on the job. We'll be ready to run that herd to the railroad in a coupla days. Slim Dryden is lending a hand and he'll help us with the drive. Everything is going to work out."

Leaving Allison in a much better frame of mind, they headed back for the spread. The sky had cleared and the low lying sun was shining brightly.

For some miles after leaving the town, the trail wound over the level rangeland, with the loom of the hills on the right and at no great distance. Then, as it drew nearer Coffin Mountain, for a mile or more it followed the crest of a hogback ridge with steeply sloping, boulder-strewn and brush-grown sides. Gradually, however, the ground on the left swelled upward until only the right-hand slope remained, with the trail edging along its lip. To the left were now scattered groves and thickets. They were passing a densely grown clump when Woodard, whose eyes constantly roved over the terrain, suddenly flung up his head, his hand dropping to his gun butt.

But even as he did so, smoke spurted from the thicket and there was the ringing crack of a gunshot. Woodard flung up his hands, reeled and fell sideways from the saddle. His body struck the lip of the trail and slid over it. Down the steep slope he rolled, amid a shower of loosened stones and sliding shale. Helpless to retard his downward progress, he slipped and bounded. He went crashing through a bristle of brush, dropped six or seven feet sheer and brought up in an earthy hollow with a bone-creaking jar. He dimly heard, through a wave of blackness that enveloped him, a terrified scream on the trail above.

6

Moonlight was streaming through the tangle of branches over his head when Jim Woodard finally came back to his senses. For several minutes he lay perfectly still, staring dazedly. Then recollection returned and he strove to sit up.

Nausea rushed over him and he slumped back, closing his eyes and fighting against the cloying sickness. It passed quickly, however, and he risked opening his eyes again. There was a dull ache in his head and he was so sore all over that it was agony to move. But on examination, he found no limb that would not function, no joint that would not bend. He managed to stagger to his feet, clutching the low growing branches for support. For a moment he stood weaving, then his head cleared and he glanced around.

He was standing under a tangle of overhanging growth which obscured his view. He scrambled out and, glancing upward, could see the lip of the trail no great distance above.

"I sure came down fast," he muttered, gingerly exploring with his fingertips a shallow ragged furrow just below the hairline above his left temple. The whole left side of his face was caked with dried blood, but he quickly decided, from various symptoms, that the wound was slight.

"The slug hit me a smart crack on the head, though," he told himself. "I've a notion if I hadn't seen the shine of the sun on the hellion's rifle barrel and thrown up my head, he woulda drilled me dead center.

Came mighty nigh it anyhow. Blazes! I wonder where is Mary?"

With quickening concern he scrambled up the slope to the trail. The full moon, high in the sky, made the scene as bright as day. Coffin Mountain loomed black and ominous, a few miles to the south. The silvery light softened and mellowed the tangle of thorny growth to the left. Ahead the trail stretched silent and deserted.

"The hellions must have done something to her," the Range Rider muttered apprehensively. "She's not the sort to sashay off and leave a jigger in the lurch. If she left here without trying to find out what happened to me, she didn't leave of her own accord."

His eyes roved over the forbidding terrain, but there was no sign of either the girl or her horse.

Abruptly a plaintive whinny sounded from nearby. Woodard pursed his lips and whistled softly. The whinny answered him and a moment later Rojo sidled out of a thicket and came toward him with a questioning air.

"Might have known the sidewinders wouldn't have been able to drop a loop on you, feller," Woodard said, thankfully stroking the red sorrel's soft muzzle. "Mighty glad they didn't plug you before yuh got outa range. What happened to the girl?"

Rojo blew softly into the Range Rider's cupped palm.

"Well," Woodard told him grimly. "I reckon it's up to you and me to find out. Thank the good Lord for that rain this afternoon. We'd oughta be able to track the hellions in this bright light."

Looping the sorrel's bridle over his arm, he set out down the trail, carefully scrutinizing the rain-softened surface.

"Here it is, feller," he exulted a moment later. "Tracks of three horses, plumb fresh. There must have been two of them, then. Riding three abreast. Mary's horse in the middle and one on each side holding onto the bit straps. Let's go, feller. With any kind of luck we'd oughta have a showdown before daylight."

For several miles he followed the triple tracks. Coffin Mountain drew nearer and nearer. Finally, where the northern slope of the great hill began, the Range Rider suddenly halted. The tracks he was following turned off to the right.

"I figgered as much," he exclaimed. "They're heading for that darn mountain. Now if the moon just doesn't get too low in the sky before we figger which way they went!"

The tracks ran west for a half a mile or more. Then abruptly they turned south and began ascending the long, growth-bristling slope of the mountain. Very soon Woodard decided they followed a distinct trail that wound up the mountain, a trail that showed signs of considerable recent usage.

"Reckon you can take over for a spell, feller," he told the sorrel, and swung into the saddle.

Up and up climbed the faint trail, little more than a game track, winding among the thorny growth and the black rocks. The moon slanted down the western sky and long shadows began creeping down the slope.

It was an eerie, desolate terrain. More than once, Woodard heard the lethal buzz of a disturbed rattlesnake. Rojo snorted, and stepped gingerly. The click of his irons on the stones sounded disquietingly loud in the silent night.

"Notion I'll hafta hole you up somewhere and go it alone before long, feller," Woodard told him, glancing upward. The crest of the mountain was still considerably more than a mile distant, but very shortly Woodard pushed the sorrel into a dense thicket that flanked the trail and tied him there. Bestowing a pat on the glossy neck, he slid back to the trail and pursued the trip on foot.

He had reached the belt of shadow, now, and his progress was slow. The ground was rough and rocky, and he had to be careful not to disturb loose stones that would roll down the slope and kick up a prodigious clatter. Slowly and painfully he groped along, peering and listening. But no sound shattered the deathly silence and he could see nothing save the encroaching growth that brandished crooked limbs against the sky and seemed to reach for him with clutching hands. The black rocks were stealthily crouching monsters waiting to pounce.

On he went, past trees that were not trees, past rocks that were not rocks, with the starry reaches of the sky above and the black mantle of the shadows below. He seemed to be swinging in a void between two fathomless immensities. Gradually he developed an uncanny feeling that he was traveling in a circle and getting nowhere. The climbing trail was endless. The sinister growth crowded closer and closer. No sound whatever blunted the sharp edge of the silence.

Then suddenly he heard sound ahead. He

halted instantly and stood with every nerve tense, straining his ears, peering into the blackness that pressed down upon him like a smothering blanket.

Again came the sound, not loud, but sharp and ringing. He catalogued it — the impatient stamp of a restless horse in the darkness ahead.

"Getting somewhere at last," he muttered, loosening his guns in their sheaths.

Slowly and with the greatest caution he crept forward. The trail appeared to have straightened out, but it was appreciably steeper. Then abruptly it leveled off and he saw a faint glow of light, so faint that it would hardly have been discernible except to eyes that had been straining at utter darkness. It might have been nothing more than the phosphorescence rising from a heap of fungus, or even from a decaying animal.

Woodard hesitated a moment, then continued his cautious advance. As he progressed, the light strengthened until it was a steady glow. Gradually it developed a symmetrical roundness. A few more minutes of slow creeping and he realized it was the glow seeping from the mouth of a lighted cave — a cave in the side of the mountain and only a little way below its crest.

The mouth of the cave was perhaps a

hundred yards from where the Range Rider crouched. The approach to it was naked rock, with the growth falling steeply away on either hand.

His eyes fixed on the glowing circle, Woodard did some hard and fast thinking. He felt sure that the men he had been trailing were holed up in the cave. Perhaps they were asleep. But then again they might be on watch just inside the entrance. There was not a particle of cover between him and the cave mouth and enough reflected moonlight fell upon the bare rock to reveal anything attempting to pass across its surface.

Woodard considered the situation. Before long the moon would be low in the sky and the darkness more profound. But he had a disquieting presentiment that to delay would be dangerous. For some moments he debated the matter with an earnestness that almost amounted to mental agony.

"I got a feeling that those two hellions came up here to wait for somebody," he told himself. "If they did, and I wait before jumping them, things are liable to be wuss than they are now. With only two hellions to deal with, I got a chance, but if the rest of the gang shows up about the time I start moving, I'll be plumb outa luck. No, I'd better risk it right now."

He made sure his guns were in perfect working order. Then setting the big sixes loosely in their sheaths, he drew a deep breath and raced across the bare space with swift, light steps. He reached the cave mouth, plunged into the lighted circle. As he did so, two men who were crouched half dozing over a small fire leaped erect with yelps of alarm. They saw the tall form of the Range Rider looming before them and went for their guns. The cave fairly exploded with the roar of six-shooters.

Five seconds later, Jim Woodard peered through the smoke wreaths at the huddled forms of the two owlhoots lying beside the fire. A burning rasp along his ribs told where a bullet had seared his flesh, but otherwise he was untouched.

Satisfied that there was nothing further to fear from the drygulchers, he took a step forward.

"Mary?" he called. "Where are you?"

"Back here," the girl's voice answered. "Oh, Jim, is that you?"

She lay on a rough bunk built against the inner wall of the shallow cave, securely bound. Woodard quickly cut the cords and chafed her numb wrists and ankles until she could stand.

"What happened?" he asked her.

"They brought me here, those two terrible men," she replied in a shaking voice. "They threatened me with their guns when I tried to speak to them. I don't know what they intended doing with me, but I was terribly frightened. I — I thought you were dead, when you went rolling down the slope."

"Just creased, and knocked out for a spell. I'm all right now," Woodard told her cheerfully. He knelt to examine the dead owlhoots.

"Apache breeds, both of them, I'd say," he decided.

He pondered the bodies, arrived at a decision.

"Mary," he said, "I'm gonna drag these hellions out and pitch 'em down the slope into the brush, out of sight. Then when we leave here we'll take their horses with us. That had oughta puzzle anybody who comes looking for this pair. You wait here a minute."

He dragged the bodies out of the cave and hurled them down the steep brush-grown slope to the right. They crashed through the growth for some distance and vanished. Then he located the horses, tethered in the shelter of an overhang on the left side of the cave. The slope here was much gentler than on the right, though just as thickly grown with brush. He returned to the girl, leading the horses.

"Okay," he told her, "we'll trail our ropes away from here. Wait till I kick this fire out."

He stamped the embers black and then led the way out of the cave. Just beyond the entrance, however, he halted.

"Listen," he warned the girl.

From the darkness below came a faint, rhythmic clicking. It was the beat of horses' irons on the stones.

"Here come some more of the same sort," growled Woodard. "Quick — around to the left and down inter the brush. If the horses will just keep still I figger we'll be all right. A good thing all the shooting was inside the cave. If it had been outside, the chances are they would have heard it."

They forced their way some distance down the slope and deep into the dense growth. With every nerve strung tensely they waited. Soon there was a clattering of hoofs on the stone above, then a rumble of harsh voices. Woodard could not overhear what was said, but it seemed to him that the voices held a querulous note.

"I've a notion they're sorta puzzled as to why that pair isn't here to meet them," Woodard told the girl. "Quiet! Somebody's coming around this way."

A thud of boot heels sounded above, then a scratching and scrambling as if somebody were climbing the steep slope that led to the mountain crest. The sounds ceased. Several minutes of silence followed, broken only by the indistinct grumble of voices in front of the cave. Then suddenly a flickering glow appeared on the mountain top. Swiftly it grew to a leaping flame that soared high into the air. Against the fierce glow they could see the tall form of a man standing with his back to them.

For some minutes the fire pulsed and blazed. Then it quickly died to a flickering glow.

"Okay," a voice called from the mountain crest. "Okay, everythin's all set."

It seemed to Woodard that the harsh tones had a familiar ring to them. He ardently wished he had caught a glimpse of the man's face. The scraping and scrambling of his descent began. Somebody voiced a question that was unintelligible to the listeners in the brush as the man joined his companions. He grunted an equally unintelligible reply.

For some little time the group conversed in front of the cave. Then there was a jingle of bridle irons and a popping of saddle leather as they mounted. Hoofs clicked across the rock and finally died away in the distance.

"We'll give them ten minutes to clear, then we'll head down the mountain, too," Woodard told the girl.

Leading her horse and the two riderless mounts, he made his way down the dark slope to where he had cached Rojo. He led the sorrel out of the thicket, forked him and together they proceeded to the level prairie and the Pasajero Trail. A couple of miles down the trail Woodard got the rigs off the two owlhoot horses, concealed them under some brush and turned the animals loose.

"They can fend for themselves all right," he told Mary. "If any of that bunch does happen to run onto them, they'll be up in the air for fair. I figger there's gonna be a lot of tall guessing as to what became of those two hombres we left up in the brush. And I wanta ask yuh to do something, Mary — don't say a word to anybody about what happened tonight."

"Of course I won't, if you say not to, Jim," she readily agreed. "But," she added demurely, "if any of the boys are awake and see us ride in together at this time of night, I wonder what *they'll* wonder?"

"Tell 'em we were doing the town together," Woodard chuckled.

"That'll be fine," Mary agreed. "That is if somebody doesn't mention what time we left town."

They laughed and let it go at that. Another mile, and they were home.

7

Late the following evening the Bar A had visitors. Old Man Stevens of the Circle S, which lay east of the Double R, rode up the Pasajero Trail. Stevens was tired, dusty and in a very bad temper. His hands, who rode with him, were in like case.

"Fifty prime beefs from my south pasture," he declared wrathfully. "We trailed the sidewinders out onto the desert, and lost 'em, of co'hse. It beats me how them hellions get out there, and then just nacherly go up in smoke. Where do they go? Where do they take the cows they rustle? Across seventy miles of desert to Mexico? It just nacherly don't make sense. And it ain't no jokin' matter. If this keeps up, the hull kit and bilin' of us in this section is gonna go bust."

"What time did they run 'em off, do yuh figger?" asked Jim Woodard.

"Sometime between midnight and mawnin', I'd say, judging from the look of the tracks," Stevens replied.

Woodard looked very thoughtful, but said nothing more.

Aside from being bruised and sore all over from his wild roll down the slope, Woodard was none the worse for the happenings of the night before. The bullet crease on his head was little more than a scratch and caused him no inconvenience. With his hat on, it did not even show. Mary Allison, also, had quickly thrown off the effects of her harrowing experience.

"Another day," Woodard told her, "and we'll have that herd ready to roll."

"I certainly hope nothing happens to it," the girl remarked anxiously. "The money those cows will bring will just about enable us to meet the payment due on that note the bank holds. I hate to think what will happen if I fail to make that payment."

"You'll make it," Woodard assured her. "This time next week those cows will be rolling east in the cars. Old Sime Price won't get his hooks in the Bar A this time."

On the morning of the second day after this conversation, the shipping herd was ready to take the trail. The Bar A outfit was augmented by nearly a dozen cowboys from the Lazy D, as well as by rotund Slim Dryden, the owner.

"Don't figger to take any chances with this one," Dryden told Woodard. "I 'low the only way us fellers hereabouts can be safe is to band up together for our drives and sich. Reckon no owlhoot outfit would take a chance on tacklin' a bunch like we got together right now, no matter how salty they might be."

"What we got to worry about most is how much savvy they got," Woodard pointed out. "They've showed plenty of wrinkles on their horns of late. We've got to be on the lookout for tricks."

"We'll trick 'em!" growled Dryden. "Jest let me line sights with one of them hellions. I'll fill him so full of holes he'll starve to death from leakin' out his vittles. Okay, boys, set 'er rollin'."

The herd did not travel by way of the Pasajero Trail, but north and east across the Double R and the Circle S, which was the more direct route to Casterville, the railroad shipping point.

Woodard was trail boss, Dryden acting as his assistant. Near the head of the trudging column of cattle on either side of the herd rode the point men who piloted the cows in the direction they wished them to go. A third of the way back came the swing riders, where the herd would begin to bend in case of a change of course. Another third of the way back were the flank riders. It was the duty of both swing and flank riders to block the cows from sideways wandering, and to drive off any foreign cattle that might try to join the herd in the course of its crossing the other spreads. Bringing up the rear were the drag riders. These last had the chore of hustling up the lazy cows that showed a tendency to lag, and to look after any that might suffer chance injury. They spent most of their time cussing the dust and recalcitrant steers that wished to go somewhere else than straight ahead. Further back were the spare horses in charge of a wrangler and rearmost of all rumbled the chuck wagon driven by the cook. Sometime during the afternoon, Woodard and Dryden would ride on ahead of the herd to choose a suitable camping spot for the night. The chuck wagon would also forge ahead and follow up the trail boss so the cook could have supper ready for the hands by the time the herd was bedded down for the night.

Woodard took the additional precaution of having outriders attend the herd. Two of these rode ahead of the herd and a half mile or a mile to one side, ranging the country, keeping a sharp lookout for anything that might appear suspicious. Two more paralleled the herd about midway back, and a final pair rode some distance to the rear, keeping a watch on the back trail.

"Best to take no chances," Woodard told Dryden. "And with yore men lending a hand, we got plenty of riders to do the thing right."

With this the Lazy D owner emphatically agreed.

"A feller who takes chances in this section, the way things have been of late, needs his head examined," Dryden declared.

All day, under a hazy sky, the herd rumbled along. The low hills to the east gradually drew near, and as the afternoon wore on, their rounded crests seemed sifted with violet dust. Far to the west, the grim battlements dominated by Coffin Mountain looked dark and angry in the reddish light of the haze-filmed sun.

"Looks like we might have fallin' weather," growled Dryden, glancing at the ominous sky. "If there's one thing I don't like durin' a drive it is lightnin'. A herd sends up lots of heat, and heat attracts lightnin'. Sometimes durin' a thunder storm I take off my slicker, even if its rainin' hard, to let my body cool. Less chance of gettin' hit then. And I allus like to wrap a rag around my guns if I can. I've knowed fellers to shuck their guns and spurs and leave 'em behind in a bad storm, but I never went that far."

Woodard smiled slightly, knowing that Dryden was voicing beliefs common among old-time cowmen. That such beliefs were nothing but superstitions with no grounding of fact, he very well knew, but he did not contradict the Lazy D owner, who was undoubtedly "sot in his ways" and difficult to change.

Late in the afternoon, when the sun was but a short distance above the western crags, the herd topped the crest of a long rise. Dryden, who, with Woodard, was riding near the head of the herd, gestured with his hand.

"Down there is the river we gotta cross," he observed. "And up there is the pass through the hills. We'll shove 'em across the river and through the pass while it's still light. Just over the other side of the pass is a fust rate place to bed 'em down for the night."

Woodard gazed in the direction the ranch owner indicated. A mile or so down the far side of the slope ran the river. It was fairly high and nearly two hundred yards in width at this point. The trail flowed up the steep far bank and on up the slope of the hills into a deep notch that split their rounded crests. The far bank was thickly covered with thorny growth that extended to the water's edge. The only break in the dense bristle was where the trail left the river. The bank was steep, almost a bluff.

"That notch is the only way yuh can get through the hills," said Dryden. "No climbin' the bank any place else for miles either way. Whoop 'em up, boys! There ain't much light left, and it looks more all the time like it was goin' to storm."

With the cowboys urging it to greater speed, the herd began streaming down the slope. The cattle didn't like the looks of the swollen river, but with the point and swing riders prodding them, the leaders took to the water. For nearly two thirds of the way across the cows kept their footing; then, as the water deepened, they began to swim. Tossing horns streaked across the yellow flood like meteors across a cloudy sky. The point men swam their horses on either side, whooping encouragement. The leaders reached the bank, clambered up it, shaking the drops from their glistening hides. They began streaming up the bank toward the notch. The main body of the herd, intent on keeping up with the leaders, redoubled their efforts.

"Not much current, which is a mighty good thing, with only that narrow stretch where they can climb the bank," Dryden observed to Woodard. "If they got swept downstream, they'd be goners."

More and more cattle lumbered up the bank. The leaders were already well up the slope toward the notch, quickening their pace as they sensed good grass on the far side of the pass. The point men drove their horses for the bank, whooping cheerily.

Their whoops changed to yells of alarm as from the dark mass of growth that fringed either side of the crossing came spurts of smoke. Even as the crack of the unseen rifles reached the watchers on the bank, one of the point men threw up his hands, reeled from the saddle and vanished beneath the surface of the yellow water. One glimpse they had of his body rolling over and over downstream, before he disappeared. The second point rider screamed with pain, lurched, wavered, gripped the horn of his saddle with one hand and frantically strove to turn his swimming horse. The swing riders had already got their horses' heads around and were surging back toward the near bank. After them came the second point man, slumped forward on his horse's neck but retaining his grip on the horn.

With yells of rage, the cowboys sent their horses racing toward the water's edge. They were met by a storm of bullets fired by the hidden riflemen. One cried out as a slug ripped the top of his shoulder. Another threw a hand to his face, which was suddenly streaked with scarlet.

"Back!" Jim Woodard roared at them. "Back out of range. Yuh got no chance against those hellions holed up out of sight! Back!"

The hands obeyed. Woodard, with slugs whining all about him, sat his horse on the edge of the bank until the last man, the wounded point rider, came clambering up the steep slope.

"Hang on with both hands," he told the injured man. Reaching out he gripped the horse's bit strap. He whirled Rojo, the slugs still whistling about their ears.

Back up the slope, the cursing cowhands were pulling their blowing horses to a halt. Gazing back over the stream, they saw the last of the herd clambering out of the water. And even as the last cow topped the bank, mounted men bulged out of the brush on either side of the trail. With snapping slickers and whirling quirts, they sent the herd bellowing up the slope.

"After the sidewinders!" bellowed Dryden. "Don't let 'em get away with it."

"Wait!" roared Woodard as the punchers sent their horses skalleyhooting back down the slope.

Scant seconds later his warning was justified. From the growth across the stream came spurts of smoke. Bullets whined about the approaching cowboys.

"Come back here!" Woodard thundered to them. "They've left men holed up in the brush to hold the ford. Yuh can't get across."

Reluctantly the enraged punchers obeyed. Woodard half drew his heavy Winchester from where it snugged in the saddle boot under his left thigh, then let it slide back into place.

"No use wasting ammunition," he said. "They're plumb out of range."

Seething with anger, the helpless outfit watched the last of the herd stream into the notch and vanish. Woodard glanced at the sun, which was almost below the western crags.

"The ones left behind will stay there and hold the ford till it gets dark. Then they'll sneak away," he told Dryden. "What kind of country beyond that pass? Have they got a good chance to give us the slip?"

"A plumb good chance," growled the ranch owner. "It's broken country over there, full of canyons and gulches, with trails nobody but the owlhoots know runnin' in every direction. We won't have the chance of a wax dog in hell runnin' 'em down in the dark. That herd's a goner."

"Mebbe not," Woodard replied quietly. He glanced at the sky. The sun was behind the western hills and the shadows were deepening. Already they could barely discern the brush-grown far bank of the stream.

The wagon had joined them and the cook was adding his curses to the others.

"You two jiggers have the cook patch yuh up," Woodard told the wounded punchers, whose hurts, he had ascertained, were not serious. "As soon as it is good and dark, make camp here. You three stay with the wagon. Keep yore eyes skun, and, though I don't think it's liable to happen, if anyone comes across that river during the night, let 'em have it plenty. As soon as it is light, swim the wagon across. Take it through the notch and hold it at the camping place over there."

He dismounted, leaned against one of the long poles which had been lashed to either side of the wagon to facilitate floating it across the stream, and rolled a cigarette.

"In ten minutes it'll be black dark," he told Dryden. "Then we're riding. By the way, isn't there a trail over there that leads down to the bay?"

"Sure there is. How in blazes did yuh guess it?" wondered Dryden. "There's an old trail that ain't used anymore — hasn't been for years. It comes out of a canyon down there to the south, less'n a mile from the water's edge."

Woodard nodded. He smoked thoughtfully for some minutes, his gaze fixed on the far bank. Soon he could distinguish nothing beyond the hurrying water. The sun had gone out like a candle. The sky above was black and there was an occasional mutter of thunder in the west.

"Time to ride," he told the hands. "Anybody watching across there can't see us."

"Yuh figger yuh know which way them hellions went?" Dryden asked.

"I do," Woodard replied briefly.

"And we're gonna chase after 'em, and run 'em down?"

Woodard shook his head. "The advantage would be all theirs then," he said. "They'll be on the lookout on the chance we may pick up their trail. No, we're riding south, on this side of the hills."

"On this side! What the — ?"

"Slim," Woodard interrupted, "I'm playing a hunch, and if it turns out to be a straight one, as I figger it will, we'll have those cows back in our hands before daylight. Let's go."

"It sounds loco to me," growled the Lazy D owner, "but mebbe yuh know what yuh're talkin' about. I'll string along with yuh."

8

The punchers, who had dropped from their saddles and were lolling on the grass, smoking, mounted again. Following Woodard's lead, they turned their horses' heads south.

Woodard led the way, setting a swift pace. The going was good, despite the darkness, and they seldom had to slow down for rough stretches. The miles flowed away behind them as the horses slogged steadily ahead. They had not been pushed during the day and were comparatively fresh.

From time to time Woodard gazed steadily into the southwest. It must have been close to midnight and the mutter of thunder that promised rain was growing to a low rumble when he saw what he had expected, sooner or later, to see.

High in the sky appeared a sudden pinpoint of light. It pulsed and wavered, grew larger, flared brightly for a few moments, then swiftly died.

"Another fire on top of Coffin Mountain," Woodard told himself. "Uh-huh, I'll bet my last peso I'm riding a straight hunch!"

None of the others had noticed the mysterious flare. Woodard did not see fit to mention it.

The hills on their left were becoming lower. Finally, a couple of hours or so after midnight, they had dwindled to a long slope running down to the level stretch that flanked the bay.

"We ought to be gettin' purty near in line with that canyon mouth yuh spoke of, hadn't we?" Woodard asked Dryden.

"Another mile or so and we can cross the river, ride another mile and be right at it," Dryden replied. "Do yuh figger that herd will come down that trail, Jim?"

"That's right."

"But in the name of blazes, why?" sputtered Dryden. "They could run 'em on east and get over inter the lake country and find places they could hole 'em up till they have a chance to dispose of 'em. By comin' down this way, they'd hafta cross miles and miles of open rangeland to get to the desert. They'd be trailin' by daylight and stand a mighty good chance of bein' spotted. It jest nacherly don't make sense."

"A lot of things that have been happening hereabouts of late don't make sense," Woodard countered grimly. "You pick the best place to ford the river, if yuh can see to do it. Getting darker all the time."

"We'll be climbin' another sag in a few minutes," Dryden said. "Down the other side of that we'll cut across the river. It's wide and shallow down here and easy to get over. I know this section purty well, and I figger to go right."

They climbed the long slope, scudded down the far side and turned sharply to the left.

"Look!" Dryden exclaimed fervently. "The clouds are breakin' a mite and we'll get a little starshine."

Soon the gleam of water showed directly ahead. Another moment and they were sloshing through the shallow stream. They rode due east, with the long slope of the hills close on their left. A mile or so farther on a dark opening yawned in the rise.

"There's the canyon mouth," said Dryden. "The trail I was tellin' yuh about comes outa it."

Flanking the canyon mouth on either side was a straggle of brush.

"Here's where we hole up," Woodard told his men. "If I'm figgering right, the hellions will be along any time now."

But a weary hour of waiting followed, and nothing happened. A second hour was drawing to a close, and the only sound audible was the distant boom of the breakers where the waters of the bay washed the rocky shoreline. The punchers began to mutter among themselves in low tones. The horses were growing restless.

And then suddenly a faint murmur of sound came from the black canyon mouth. It swiftly grew in volume until the listeners recognized it to be the moan of tired, disgusted cattle. A barely audible clicking swelled to a low rumble of many hoofs.

"Get set," Woodard told the cowboys.

The noise of the approaching cattle increased until it vibrated the canyon walls. A dark mass appeared, dimly seen in the faint starlight. It rolled past with a clashing of horns and pounding of hoofs. On the heels of the churning herd came shadowy horsemen. Jim Woodard's voice rang out.

"Give them hell!"

Instantly the fringe of brush flanking the canyon mouth blazed with gunfire. The cattle bellowed with fright and scattered wildly. Screams of pain and yells of terror filled the air. It was blind shooting in the almost pitch dark, but three saddles were emptied by that first roaring volley.

The owlhoots fired back wildly, howled, cursed, fought with their maddened horses. Then, as a deadly storm of lead continued to whistle around them, they wheeled their terrified mounts and went tearing back into the blackness of the canyon.

Woodard sent Rojo surging forward. His whooping men raced after him. But before they reached the canyon mouth, they were engulfed in the churning herd. It took them minutes to untangle themselves.

"Hold it!" Woodard shouted. "It's no use. The hellions have got too much of a start. They'll take to the brush when they hear us coming. Let them go, and start getting those cows together before they break their necks or drown themselves."

It took a lot of hard work to turn the stampeding herd and get it to milling. However, the cows were about worn out, and once they were well massed they settled down to feeding.

"We'll hold them here until daylight," Woodard said. "Then we'll run them back up that trail."

He turned and stared long and earnestly toward the bay, but nothing was visible save the phosphorescent gleam of the wave crests rolling in to break on the rocks.

"Any chance of them sidewinders comin' back?" Dryden wondered.

"Not them," Woodard chuckled in reply. "I figger they got a bellyful. Reckon this was the last thing they allowed to happen."

"And gettin' those cows back is the last thing *I* 'lowed to happen," grunted Dryden. "I still can't see how yuh figgered it out."

"Let's have a look at the three we downed," Woodard suggested. "Might as well light a fire over there under the cliff. It's none too warm down here close to the water. We'll drag the bodies up to it and give them a once-over."

The cowboys scanned the bodies of the slain wideloopers. "Never seed any of 'em before. Ornery lookin' hellions," was the general comment.

"Wait a minute, though," Slim Dryden suddenly exclaimed. "I've seed that lanky one some place. Let me think, now. I got it! I got him spotted now. He usta be a bartender over to Dynham. Worked for old Si Mason in his Dust Settler saloon. Got hisself appointed deputy town marshal at Dynham. Went on a drunk a coupla weeks ago and they fired him. Left town, I understand. Said he was goin' on a trip."

"Uh-huh, he's started on a long one, from the looks of him right now," growled one of

Dryden's punchers. "Reckon he'll end up in a hotter climate than Nueces county can dish out."

"Deputy town marshal at Dynham, eh?" Woodard remarked. "That's the mining town to the west of Lorenzo, isn't it?"

"That's right," Dryden agreed. "A purty salty pueblo, pertickler on paydays. Wouldn't be over surprised if some of this wideloopin' gang are from there. I don't spot nothin' familiar about the other two, though. Scrubby lookin' horned toads. Nothin' about 'em to make 'em stand out in a crowd."

Nor did the pockets of the unsavory trio divulge anything of particular interest. They wore ordinary range garb. Their horses were rounded up with considerable difficulty and proved to be good enough stock but nothing exceptional. All three bore intricate Mexican brands that were not recognized by anybody present. The rigs were average and showed signs of much use.

"It's an out-of-the-section outfit, all right, rangin' over here from some place," declared Dryden. "Mebbe from down *mañana* way. Them other two hellions has a sorta oiler look to me. Don't you think so, Jim?"

"More liable to be breeds with a considerable dash of Apache blood, I'd say," Woodard replied.

Taking turns at night-hawking, the cowboys managed to get some sleep around the fire. Daybreak found them on the move. They shoved the herd into the canyon and drove north, following the old trail that wound through the hills.

"She was used plenty once, a long, long time ago," Woodard told Dryden.

"I been told the old freebooters who used to maverick around the bay made it runnin' the stuff they stole from the Dons up to San Antonio," Dryden said. "As I understand it, them old fellers were a sort of water-goin' wideloopers. They handled a slick iron, all right, if the stories I've heard are anythin' like true."

"I've a notion they left some descendants who wear the same brand," Woodard stated cryptically.

Dryden stared at him questioningly, but the Range Rider did not see fit to amplify the remark.

Woodard and Dryden rode ahead of the drive, watchful and alert, but they saw nothing suspicious.

"Haven't any notion much those hellions would try something else, but it's best not to take chances," said the former.

"Yuh're right," Dryden agreed. "I don't

put nothin' past that outfit."

Woodard was ready to agree. "But like all the breed, they slip up on little things," he told his companion.

"Mebbe," the other replied dubiously, "but I ain't seen no evidence of it so far. It was just a case of you outsmartin' the sidewinders, the way I see it. That trap they laid for us at the river was a lulu. I 'lowed I'd figgered on everythin', but that one was plumb new."

"Yes, they put one over on all of us there," Woodard admitted. "We'd oughta figgered that crossing would be just the place for a drygulching, but I'm darned if I know what we coulda done about it, unless we'd sent men ahead to guard it the day before."

"I've a notion if yuh'd knowed about it, that is just what yuh woulda done," Dryden replied. "I'd oughta told yuh more."

"And I'd oughta asked yuh more perticklers about the route we'd travel," Woodard shouldered his share of the blame. "Well, if it wasn't for that pore devil of a point man who rode his last river, there wouldn't have been much harm done."

"The hellions paid three for one for him," Dryden reminded grimly. "That ain't such a bad trade."

"One honest man is wuth the whole

ornery outfit," Woodard disagreed.

Glancing at his companion, Dryden saw that Woodard's green eyes had subtly changed color. They were icy gray, the color of the cold waters of the bay beating the shoreline under a cloudy winter sky.

"And I got a notion that outfit ain't really started payin' yet," he told himself. "I'd rather have somethin' outa hell on my trail than this big jigger."

9

Late in the afternoon the herd reached the spot where the Casterville trail crossed the ancient track of the freebooters. They found the chuck wagon awaiting them. For some time the cook was the busiest man in the section, and the famished cowboys did full justice to his "dishin's out."

That night the herd bedded down where it had expected to the night before, and by mid afternoon of the following day it rolled into Casterville where it was speedily taken over by the buyer who awaited it, and payment collected.

"Reckon Miss Mary will be able to sorta tangle old Sime Price's twine for him after all," Woodard observed with satisfaction.

As he and Dryden entered a restaurant

for a bite to eat, Woodard was surprised to encounter Carter Renshaw in company with Preston Grimes, the new owner of the Rambler saloon at Lorenzo. Both looked tired and dusty and showed other signs of hard riding.

"My herd gets in tomorrow," Renshaw explained to Dryden. "Figgered I'd amble over and be here to meet it. Grimes came along with me. He's figgerin' on buyin' a ranch in the section, if he can get one, and sorta wants to get onto the business."

"Never was in the cattle business," Grimes amplified, "but it looks to me like a good investment."

"If it's run right, and yuh have some luck," grunted Dryden.

Woodard speculated as the pair departed, Grimes striding lithely and Renshaw keeping pace with him with his peculiar rolling gait.

"Looks like those hombres aren't on the prod against each other like they were at fust," he remarked.

"Oh, I reckon they decided there weren't no sense in pawin' the hackamore," Dryden replied. "Cart allus struck me as bein' level headed, even though he has got a flashy temper, and I've a notion Grimes don't let puhsonal feelin's stand in his way when a dollar is to be made. He's sorta got the look. Looks more like a gambler than anythin' else. Not the tinhorn sort, but the kind what handles big games where the stakes are high. Yeah, I've a notion he's shuffled a pasteboard or two in his time."

Woodard had something of the same notion, and he was very thoughtful in the course of the long ride back to the Bar A ranchhouse.

Three days later, Woodard and Mary Allison visited the Lorenzo bank. Old Sime Price received them in his private office. He glanced keenly at Woodard when Mary introduced the Range Rider as her foreman, but his greeting was cordial enough.

"We will handle the transaction this time," he said, when Mary took up the matter of the mortgage payment on the spread. "I'm glad to say," he added, putting the fingertips of his wrinkled hands together and pursing his lips, "that the Lorenzo bank no longer owns the notes in question. We recently disposed of them to a buyer who evidently considered them a better investment than we do."

"You sold the mortgage!" Mary exclaimed. "Who to?"

Price wagged his hard-looking head. "To a newcomer in the section, who seems to want to get into the cattle business," he said. "We sold it to Preston Grimes, the new owner of the Rambler saloon."

Mary Allison regarded him in stunned silence for a moment. Finally she drew a deep breath.

"And I suppose," she said bitterly, "that part of the payment was in the blood money Ward Grimes received for murdering my brother."

Old Sime wagged his head again, and clucked disapprovingly.

"Now, Miss Mary," he protested, "yuh have no call to feel that way. After all, Ward Grimes only did his duty as a citizen. And paid for it with his life," he added grimly.

"It was murder, pure and simple," the girl declared. "My brother never came into this bank to rob it, and you know it as well as I do."

Price shifted uncomfortably in his chair, and it seemed to Woodard that an expression of disquiet showed in his filmy eyes.

"The coroner's jury exonerated Grimes," he said, almost defensively.

"I've a notion you influenced the jury," Mary replied.

"Yuh're makin' a mighty serious charge there," Price expostulated.

"And before everything is finished, I'll

prove it," the girl declared. "Oh, I don't mean to say that you deliberately told the jurymen what to do, but your opinion in the matter was well known, and most everybody in this section is beholden to you or your bank in one way or another."

Sime Price's gaze shifted uneasily away from her steady eyes. He tugged at his low collar as if it were suddenly too tight.

"My conscience is clear," he muttered.

"But just the same, I think you are learning that a dead man doesn't make a soft pillow at night," the girl returned meaningly.

Jim Woodard with difficulty suppressed a grin. Price was visibly sweating now and was undoubtedly not enjoying the interview.

"By the way," Woodard remarked casually, speaking for the first time, "I heard a report about that killing over at Dynham. Yuh know, the miner who was killed in an alley back of the bank there. The report said he had a half stick of dynamite and a length of fuse on him. But it came out that no dynamite cap was found on him. Funny a feller would go to blow a bank vault and not take a cap to explode the dynamite. Mighty careless of him."

"Mebbe he lost it," muttered Price.

"And those two Mexicans who were killed in front of the Armstrong bank," Woodard pursued. "Yuh rec'lect they claimed to the marshal that they were waiting to meet a man there. Well, not long after they were cashed in, a rancher showed up in town trying to locate a couple of oilers he aimed to hire to do some work on his spread. Wonder if those two bank robbers could have been the fellers he was looking for?"

"You seem mighty well informed as to what's goin' on around here," Price growled, glaring at the Range Rider.

"Oh, it's purty general talk," Woodard deprecated. "In fact, I've heard folks wondering if there might not have been a mistake made in some of those reward killings."

Old Sime's face set in stubborn lines.

"I don't care to discuss the matter any furthers," he growled. "Yore receipt will be ready for yuh in a minute, Miss Mary. Yuh can make yore next payment — when yuh make it — to Preston Grimes. The bank has nothin' more to do with the business."

"Why wasn't I notified of the sale of the mortgage?" Mary asked.

"A mortgage of that nature is collateral," Price replied. "It can be sold or transferred without the knowledge of the mortgagee. We would have notified yuh, sooner or later, as a matter of business courtesy, but we

116

were not required to, under the law."

Woodard chuckled as they left the bank together.

"I've a notion that old gent isn't as easy in his mind as he'd like to be," he remarked to Mary.

"I've a notion he's beginning to learn that folks who take the law inter their own hands are shouldering a hefty chore, and one that doesn't make for easy carrying."

While Mary went to the sheriff's office to visit her father, Woodard dropped into the Rambler saloon. He noted that Preston Grimes was not in evidence at the end of the bar.

"Oh, he's out gallivantin' around somewhere," the sociable barkeep replied to Woodard's question. "He does a heap of ridin' around. Says he's lookin' over rangeland hereabouts. Understand he has a hankerin' to buy a spread."

"Mebbe he's trying to get his brother's death off his mind," Woodard conjectured.

The barkeep grunted. "Mebbe," he replied. "But if he feels over bad about Ward's passin' on, he shore don't show it. I got a notion that jigger ain't got no feelin's much of any kind. He's a cold proposition, or I never saw one. Different from Ward that way. Ward was sociable. He was salty, all right, but he got along with most everybody. That's what allus made it seem so funny to me about him killin' young Tom Allison. Him and Tom allus got along. He said afterward that he didn't know it was Tom when he shot, and I believe he was tellin' the truth, otherwise he wouldn't have shot him. He said he heard the cashier yell and when he whirled around he jest saw a feller at the window reachin' for a gun. Never occurred to him it was Allison, or anybody else he knew. Said he just throwed down on the jigger without hardly lookin'. Seems he'd oughta seen Tom go inter the bank. He went in right after him. I know that for certain."

"How?" Woodard asked, interested.

"It was like this," replied the barkeep. "I rec'lect everythin' that happened that mornin'. Young Tom was in here — playin' poker over to that corner table. He went bust in the game and come over to the bar for a drink. He finished his drink and sidled down to the end of the bar where Ward Grimes was standin'. Him and Ward talked a minute, then they went inter the back room together. A little bit later Ward came out and asked for the pen and ink and a blotter we keep in that drawer under the till in case somebody might want to write a letter or somethin', which don't often happen but does now and then. He took the stuff inter the back room and a minute or two later Tom Allison comes out and heads for the door. Sorta weaves through 'em out onto the street, I rec'lect. Musta been drunker than he looked. He'd hardly got outside before Ward comes outa the back room, puts the pen and ink in the drawer and picks up the sack we'd put the night's take in. Told me he was goin' over to the bank to deposit it. That's what makes me say he musta gone inter the bank right behind Tom Allison. Musta seed him walkin' down the street. Reckon he was busy thinkin' about things and never noticed. If he had, I got a feelin' Tom Allison would be alive today and all this trouble wouldn't never busted loose."

Woodard nodded, but did not comment. "Yuh say yuh got that writing material handy?" he remarked a little later. "Got paper and envelopes, too? I'd like to write a letter myself."

"Shore," replied the accommodating barkeep. "Go over to that vacant table in the corner."

For some time Woodard busied himself at the table with pen and paper. Finally he addressed and sealed the envelope. Then, while the barkeep was busy at the back bar, he got up and left the room. A few minutes later the drink juggler glanced around and noted the vacant table.

"Hey," he called to a swamper, "that cowboy feller went off and left the pen and ink on the table. Bring 'em here before somebody tips over the bottle.

"Where's the blotter?" he asked when the swamper passed the articles across the bar. "It's the only one we got."

"Didn't see no blotter," the swamper replied.

"Somebody musta picked it up," grunted the barkeep, stowing the pen and ink away. "We'll hafta buy a new one."

That night, in his room at the Bar A ranchhouse, Jim Woodard carefully examined the blotter in question. He crossed the room and held it before the mirror above the bureau. For some minutes he intently studied the reflection in the glass. Then, with an exclamation of satisfaction, he carefully stowed the blotter away.

"It's tying up," he muttered, an exultant glow in his green eyes. He pondered the letter he had written and mailed, a letter addressed to "Captain Mort Quigley, Cattleman's Protective Association."

"Now if I just get the answer I'm expecting!" he mused.

10

As foreman of the spread, Woodard could largely order his movements to suit himself. The following day found him riding south across the range. Where the growth thinned out and the wide stretch sparsely grown with salt grass began, he pulled Rojo to a halt and for some time sat studying the dreary expanse.

East and west stretched the flat monotony, hemmed in on either side by the hills. To the south were the tossing waters of the bay, edged by a ribbon of white that was breakers pounding the rocky coastline.

No animal moved over the level floor. A few gulls, soaring high overhead, were the only signs of life. The wind set up an eerie rustling in the tall grass and to his ears came the low mutter of the distant breakers. Far to the northwest, Coffin Mountain glowered grim and ominous against the sky. Due west, where the hills fell away, was the desert, with the sand devils dancing across it and the sunlight shimmering its gray surface.

The whole vista was one of frank poverty, of a barren wasteland with nothing to justify its existence. Just the same, Woodard felt sure that somewhere here was the key to the mystery he sought to solve.

Speaking to Rojo, he sent the sorrel slowly in the direction of the bay. Where wind and rain had washed away the thin skim of eroded topsoil, the earth beneath showed gray and lifeless, with a dusty look as of desiccated bones.

These barren patches interested the Range Rider strangely. Finally he dismounted beside one, took out his knife and began digging into the gray surface, driving the blade deep into the earth until he had a considerable hole hollowed out. He examined the dusty looking gray soil with great care, sifting it through his hands, rubbing particles between his fingertips, even tasting it. Finally he scooped up several handfuls from the bottom of the hole and stowed them in one of his saddlebags. He stared thoughtfully across the barren expanse.

"It's an arid country," he mused. "Allus has been. There are weeks in summer when the Nueces is dry as a bone for miles. Rainfall is very light, and there is no water flowing down from the slopes of the hills to wash the soluble salts into the sea. Perfect conditions to encourage efflorescence. No water to cause crystallization and the stuff changes to a powder on top of the salt, which sinks lower. Mebbe I'm wrong about it, but I don't think I am. Easy to find out for sure. These specimens go to the State University laboratory pronto."

Remounting, the concentration furrow deep against his black brows, he rode on to the water's edge.

Here he again sat his horse for some time, gazing over the sun-drenched bay, intently studying the coastline. He turned Rojo's head and rode westward along the shore, always keeping close to the water's edge.

He passed the southernmost slopes of the hills and rode out onto the shimmering desolation of the desert. As he progressed, the heat sensibly increased. The wind stirred the powdery sand and swirled it aloft in choking clouds. Soon he and his horse were both thickly powdered with gray dust. The sun was a sullen orange ball shooting its baleful rays through the veil of dust and haze.

"We're taking a chance, feller," he told his horse. "If it happens to start storming we mightn't last long."

For several miles the shoreline remained the same — jagged rocks with the surf pounding over them. Long bars extended out into the bay, over which the waves spouted geysers of foam.

As he progressed the wind dropped somewhat. The dust clouds settled. But high in the air, the finer particles still whirled and eddied. Far away he could still dimly see the mighty bulk of Coffin Mountain looming through the haze.

Gradually the shoreline changed. Smooth, sandy beaches took the place of rocks. The roar of the waters dulled to a mutter. The water changed color. Finally, several miles out on the desert, he came to a deep cove. Here the water was a deeper blue, denoting considerable depth. The ground swelled upward on both sides so that the cove was landlocked and sheltered. The waves ran in smoothly with little sound.

Woodard paused and surveyed the scene. He turned and gazed toward the mountain looming against the sky. He turned again, ran his eyes across the expanse of smooth, deep water.

"A perfect set-up," he mused, "with that darned mountain in plain view. I believe we've hit it, Rojo. Well, this is a new wrinkle in widelooping. Everything is beginning to tie up fine. All we need is a good chance to twirl our loop, but I've a notion getting that chance is going to be a considerable chore. This is going to take some thinking out.

Well, guess we'd better be heading for home. We've done all we can out here, and the wind is beginning to rise again."

He was glad indeed when he finally reached the end of the gray desolation and the fertile rangeland again rolled before him. He rode on until he hit the Pasajero Trail and turned north, glancing from time to time at the ominous mountain shouldering the sky.

No one was better pleased over the recovery of the widelooped Bar A herd than Sheriff Woll Baylor. He congratulated Woodard warmly when the Range Rider dropped in to see him a few days later.

"Yuh got the makin's of a good peace officer, son," he declared. "If yuh ever get tired of punchin' cows, let me know. I could use a smart, hustlin' deputy about yore size."

"I'll think it over," Woodard agreed smiling slightly. "By the way, Sheriff, wasn't that jigger Slim Dryden recognized — the former deputy marshal at Dynham — the feller who collected a reward for killing a miner he allowed was aiming to blow the bank vault there?"

"By gosh, that's right," exclaimed the sheriff. "Right after he got the reward money he went on a big drunk and they fired him. He sobered up a bit and left town. Went to the bad altogether, it 'pears."

"Looks that way," Woodard agreed. "Well, so long, Sheriff. I'm going down to the post office. Got a package I want to mail. Be seeing yuh. Tell Crane Allison hello for me when he wakes up."

"That hellion spends most of his time sleepin'," the sheriff growled in injured tones. "He's gettin' fat, and I'm wastin' away to a shadow. Some folks have all the luck!"

Woodard repaired to the post office, where he mailed the sample of earth he had dug from the salt flats on the south Bar A range. After that he dropped in at the Rambler saloon for a bite to eat. Preston Grimes was at his accustomed place at the far end of the bar. Carter Renshaw and his foreman, Peaseley Wallace, were playing poker at a nearby table. Renshaw nodded cordially to the Ranger. Preston Grimes also nodded, but Wallace, after casting a glowering glance in Woodard's direction, immediately turned back to his cards.

"Got a notion that red-faced gent just nacherly doesn't like anybody," the Range Rider chuckled.

As Woodard stepped into the street, shortly afterward, his attention was attracted by a clatter of fast hoofs. Glancing up the street he saw a sweat-streaked horse foaming toward him. It bore no saddle and the man who forked its bare back controlled it by means of a broken strap secured to one bit iron.

The man himself was in a condition to attract considerable attention. He was wild-eyed and haggard. His face was smeared with blood and his left arm swung limply from the shoulder. Reeling and swaying, he flashed past Woodard and hauled his horse to a skating halt in front of the sheriff's office. He slumped off the animal's back like a sack of old clothes, gripping the horse's mane for support, steadied himself an instant, then floundered up the steps and through the door.

Woodard headed for the sheriff's office at a fast pace. He entered just in time to hear the man, who was slumped in a chair, gasping out his story.

The Casterville stage, he declared, had rolled out of Dynham at eight o'clock in the morning. It would take most of the day to cover the forty-odd miles from Dynham to the railroad town. Dynham, preeminently a mining community, perched on a shelf of the range of hills that flowed northward, west of Lorenzo. A long, irregular spur of the hills fanged eastward for nearly twenty miles, falling away to slopes and rolling rangeland just north of Lorenzo. Out of Dynham the trail ran through the hills, which were steep and rocky and thickly covered with growth. Chaparral consisting largely of mesquite, prickly pear and dagger predominated, but flanking the trail at times were considerable stands of fairly heavy timber. The trail, boulder strewn and rutted, followed the path of least resistance and took its time getting through the hills.

Old Owen Hartsook, the driver, had perched comfortably on his high seat and handled his six mettlesome horses with expert ease. Beside him sat his shotgun guard, a rifle within easy reach, a lethal sawed-off resting across his knees. For the stage at times carried valuable mail and express and a guard always rode attendance.

There had been no passengers this particular trip. The mail sacks and a negligible amount of express matter were locked inside the body.

As a matter of long habit, Hartsook and the guard had kept a close eye on their surroundings as the coach wound its way through the hills. Hartsook's old Forty-four was within easy reach of his hand, and he knew how to use it. Both he and his guard had a reputation of being plumb salty hombres, and the stage had never been held up.

But the chief reason it remained unmolested, most folks said, was because it wasn't really worth bothering with. It was always highly problematical whether the mail and express it carried was of any particular value, and only a trusted few knew of what else the coach packed on occasion, and which was never in evidence or open to the glance of a casual observer.

The coach climbed a long slope, paused at the crest to breathe the horses, and then rolled smartly down the opposite sag. Hartsook kept a tight grip on the reins, while the guard cradled his shotgun across his lap and rolled a cigarette. Hartsook was always glad to get through the dense stand of thicket that hemmed the whole length of the trail up the slope. Down the sag and across the level the growth was sparse, affording little concealment. Tall trees stood at intervals, spreading their giant boughs across the trail. The sunlight made green and gold shadows on the gray dust and the air was full of the musical sough of leaves and branches in a brisk wind.

The stage reached the level ground. Old Hartsook eased off on his team and relaxed on his perch. The wheels clashed and clattered over the boulders that studded the surface of the rutted track. Hartsook opened his lips to make some inconsequential remark.

The guard never heard what he had to say. Hartsook's voice was drowned in an explosive crackling followed by a rushing roar. He yelled in terror and threw up his arm to shield his face.

On the right-hand side of the trail a great tree leaned out of the perpendicular, seemed to hang in mid air for a paralyzed second. Then it rushed downward with a mighty splitting and crashing. With a rending boom, the huge trunk struck the body of the coach, crushing it like an eggshell beneath a hammer. The wheels flew off, the body thudded to the ground. The horses snorted with terror and plunged against the breast bands. Down went one of the leaders in a flurry of kicking hoofs. In an instant the team was in a mad tangle. But the stout chain traces resisted and they were held to the wrecked coach, floundering and screaming.

Old Owen Hartsook, slashed across the face and head by a flailing branch, was hurled to the ground and lay with arms widespread, his face a bloody mass. The guard was also unseated by the shock. He landed on hands and knees and strove to rise.

From a bristle of growth behind the fallen tree surged a half dozen men, their faces swathed in black handkerchiefs cut with eyeholes. They rushed toward the stage. One flung up a gun and shot the guard squarely between the eyes. He slumped to the ground and lay still.

Another lined sights with the fallen driver, but did not pull trigger, after a glance at his motionless form and blood drenched face.

"He's done for," Hartsook heard him growl. "No sense in wastin' a ca'tridge. Smash them doors open and get to work."

Several of the men crowding behind him bore axes. With a few swinging blows they smashed in one of the doors. Then without an instant's hesitation they went to work on the floor boards of the coach, cutting and hacking with the axes.

The floor boards were an inch of seasoned oak and resisted the assault. Also, the huge tree trunk, smashed clear through the roof and upper sides of the coach hampered their efforts. Swearing and sweating, they slashed and pounded at the heavy boards. Finally one splintered. Another sagged inward, cut clear through. A man with a crowbar shoved his way into the coach, thrust the end of the bar through an opening and heaved mightily. The board creaked, groaned, gave with a sharp splintering. A dark opening yawned.

"Here it is!" whooped the man who wielded the bar. "Hit 'er a couple more licks and let me pry another plank loose. Okay, that's done it. Stand by to take the stuff."

Thrusting his arms through the opening, grunting and panting with the strain, he hauled forth a ponderous ingot, frosty white in appearance. It was a silver brick from the Dynham silver mines, with a gold content of almost one-fourth its weight. Another and another followed.

More floor boards were ripped loose, laying bare the secret compartment in which snugged the treasure-trove of the coach. More and more ingots came forth.

A string of pack mules were led out of the brush, the ingots loaded into the rawhide aparejos on their backs.

"That's the crop," called the tall masked man who directed operations. "Start 'em movin'. We haven't any time to waste."

Horses were led out of the brush. Without a glance at the still forms in the dust, the owlhoots mounted and, driving the loaded mules before them, headed south over a faint track that wound through the growth. The stage, with its trembling horses huddled in their tangled harness, lay like a squashed bug under the ponderous trunk of the fallen tree.

11

"They figgered I was done for, and I reckon I looked it, all covered with blood, like I was," old Owen Hartsook finished his story. "Anyhow, they didn't come over to finish me. But I didn't even lose my senses. Reckon the pain in my busted arm was too sharp at fust and kept me awake. I lay there with a slit between my eyelids and saw everythin' that went on. What I can't figger is how them hellions knew we were carryin' that metal. Not a half dozen folks was supposed to know about it. The stage was loaded at night. Yesterday the wagon supposed to be packin' the monthly cleanup rolled outa Dynham with guards and everythin'. She was loaded, too, with bars of lead — and anybody snoopin' around coulda seed the loadin' takin' place. But them hellions weren't fooled a mite. They went right for that false bottom in the coach. Knowed right where to look. There was a leak some place, all right, and there's gonna be hell about it. That haul ran close to forty thousand dollars, I'd say."

The sheriff swore wearily. Jim Woodard, who had listened intently to the driver's story, spoke for the first time.

"What was the weight of the metal they got?" he asked.

"There was twelve fifty-pound bars," the driver replied.

"Six hundred pounds," Woodard translated. "How many mules did they have?"

"I saw four," said Hartsook.

"A hundred and fifty pounds per mule," Woodard mused. "That's a heavy load to pack over hill trails. They couldn't make much speed."

"They got a good start, though," said Hartsook. "After they hightailed I really passed out. Was out for hours, and then I hadda ride the fifteen miles here. Yeah, they got a plumb good start."

"We're ridin' up there pronto," the sheriff said. "How many of the sidewinders did yuh say there was, Owen?"

"I counted seven," the driver replied. "There mighta been more back in the brush, but I don't think so. I reckon seven was the right number, all right. There was three big tall ones and four others sorta medium sized."

"They all wore masks?"

"That's right. Their faces was plumb

covered up."

A number of men, attracted by Hartsook's dramatic arrival, had crowded into the sheriff's office. Among them were Baylor's two deputies.

"I'd like you to go along, too, if yuh will, Jim," the sheriff said to Woodard. "And I'll swear you in, too, Blaine Evans, and you, McGregor. You three with Pete and Cary had oughta be enough to handle seven if we run 'em down. I allus favor small posses. Yuh can travel better that way, so long as yuh got jiggers yuh can depend on. Yeah, six of us will be plenty. Get the rigs on yore cayuses and let's hit the trail. Not over much daylight left. Get goin'! Some of you fellers here take Hartsook over to Doc's office and get him patched up."

Ten minutes later, the sheriff, grim of face and hard of eye, thundered out of town at the head of his posse.

The fifteen miles to the scene of the holdup were covered at a fast clip, despite the roughness of the road. Considerably less than two hours had passed when the posse pulled their blowing horses to a halt beside the wrecked stage. The dead guard lay where he had fallen, his blood-smeared face buried in the dust. Hartsook had cut the horses loose before riding for town and they were grazing near the trail.

Woodard examined the fallen tree. Quickly he discovered a stout rope tied high up on the trunk and dangling through the welter of splintered branches.

"They cut the trunk almost through," he told Sheriff Baylor. "From the look of the stump, I figger the tree nacherly leaned toward the trail. They anchored it with the rope before they started chopping. Then when the stage came along, they cut the rope and down she came. Took some careful figgering. They musta watched the coach go by a number of times and figgered just how fast it would be liable to travel. An outfit with plenty of savvy, all right. Here's where they trailed inter the brush. Not much of a track, but on this soft ground we had oughta be able to follow them. Let's go, gents. Goin' to be dark before long."

For several miles they had little trouble following the track of the heavily laden mules. But as the sun hovered over the western crags, they crossed a long ridge and their troubles began.

Beyond was a series of valleys, running this way and that. The soil was hard and stony and hoofmarks became increasingly scarce. There was no way of telling just which one of the valleys the fugitives might have followed. The sun sank behind the hills and the blue gloom of the dusk filled the depressions. Finally Sheriff Baylor pulled up, growling an oath.

"It's no use," he said. "The hellions mighta turned any direction here. It begins to look like they've give us the slip."

Jim Woodard was studying the terrain.

"Sheriff," he said, "you know the section. Is there a way to get to the Pasajero Trail from here?"

"I reckon I can figger a way," Baylor returned. "Why?"

"Because," Woodard said slowly, "I got a hunch I know where those owlhoots are heading. If my hunch is straight, we'll have them and the metal coralled before morning."

"Yuh really figger yuh can lead us to their hole-up?" Baylor exclaimed excitedly.

"Yes," Woodard replied, "I think I can. They've got to hole that metal up somewhere for a while. It takes some arranging to dispose of a haul like that. Yuh can't just walk up to an assay office and sell the stuff. If it was loose dust or nugget gold, it would be different. But molded bars could only come from a stamp mill cleanup, and an assay office would want an explanation as to where it came from and its history. They can get rid of it, all right, but only with considerable conniving. I figger they'll hold it under cover for a while. The report will go out on that holdup and every legitimate source of disposal will be on the lookout for it."

"Okay," said the sheriff. "Yuh're the bully boy with the glass eye from here on. Let's go."

Following the sheriff's directions, the posse turned and retraced their steps for a mile or more. They scrambled their horses down a long slope that led to the floor of the canyon that ran due east. Through this they stumbled in almost total darkness and finally reached the open rangeland. The sheriff led the way on a long diagonal and, glimmering wanly in the starlight, the Pasajero lay before them. Woodard turned Rojo south and they rode swiftly along the trail, toward the dark bulk of Coffin Mountain.

They crossed the hogback where Woodard was drygulched. The Range Rider intently scanned the vista ahead and finally spotted where he had turned off following the trail of the two owlhoots who carried off Mary Allison.

"Keep yore eyes skun and yore ears open from here on," he cautioned the others. "It's a salty outfit with plenty of savvy. If they get the drop on us we won't enjoy it. I figger it's going to be a case of shoot fust and ask questions afterward."

Soon they were following the narrow, brush-flanked tracks that led up the mountain. Woodard used the horses as long as he deemed it safe to do so. Then he dismounted his followers and led the way on foot.

After what seemed an endless period of climbing the steep trail, slowly and cautiously, with the greatest care not to dislodge a loose boulder or snap a twig, they reached a point where they were able to peer over the crest of the slope and across the flat expanse of rock. A glow of light met their gaze.

"Right!" Woodard breathed exultantly. "They're in the cave. Now to get to them before they line sights with us."

Crouched in the growth at the lip of the rise, the possemen studied the terrain. Woodard had little hope of catching the occupants of the cave drowsing this time. They had doubtless arrived at their hole-up but a short time before. As he hesitated what course to pursue, there drifted to his nostrils the aroma of boiling coffee.

"The hellions are cooking up a s'rounding of chuck," he breathed to his companions. "That means they're wide awake. They'll spot us sure if we try to slide across that naked rock. I figger our only chance is to sneak around to the left through the brush and come at them that way. If we make a racket doing it, they'll be ready and waiting for us. Take yore time, and don't make any slips."

With the silent stealth of an Indian, he led the way into the brush. The gloom was intense, the going difficult. A great part of the way they crawled on hands and knees between the stems of the chaparral and their progress was very slow. Occasionally, through breaks in the growth, they could see the dark crest of the mountain looming starkly against the star-burned sky. Now and then they heard the impatient stamp of horses tethered in the shelter of the over-hang, and once the raucous bray of a mule shattered the silence and set their pulses hammering with the unexpectedness of the sound.

"About time to head up the slope," Woodard whispered. "Get together under the overhang, where the horses are tied, then around the bulge and inter the cave with a rush. Guns out and ready. We'll give 'em a chance; if they won't take it, it's up to them to take something else."

Slowly and with the utmost caution, the

posse climbed the slope. One by one they slid from the growth and gathered in the darkness under the overhang.

"Get set," Woodard breathed. "Okay? Let's go!"

At a swift run he led the way around the shoulder of cliff. He was inside the cave, the sheriff and the others close at his heels, before its occupants had any notion of what was happening.

"In the name of the State of Texas!" thundered Sheriff Baylor. "Reach for the sky! Yuh're kivered!"

Hardly had the words left his lips before Jim Woodard was shooting with both hands. The four men squatted beside the fire had leaped to their feet with yelps of alarm, guns out and blazing.

Woodard saw the flash of the owlhoots' shots, felt his own Colts bucking in his hands. Lead was whining and hissing around him. A man behind him gave a cry of pain. The reports of his companions' guns roared in his ears.

In split seconds it was over. The four owlhoots lay sprawled on the floor of the cave, dead or dying. One posseman had a punctured upper arm. Another bled from a slight flesh wound in his hip.

Woodard stirred the fire to a brighter

blaze. The dead men were dragged within the circle of its light and carefully examined. They were swarthy men, all of them. One was almost black in coloring, with a broad face, a cruel gash of a mouth and high cheek bones. His hair was lank, and dead black.

"Breeds," remarked one of the deputies. "They got plenty of Injun blood. I'd say this chunky one is a almost pure-blood 'Patchy."

"Apache blood in all of them, from the look of them," Woodard supplemented.

Sheriff Baylor tugged thoughtfully at his mustache.

"Funny to find 'Patchys way over here," he remarked. "They belong in the mountain country over west. Can't say as I ever rec'lect seein' one here in the Nueces country before. Now if this was the Guadalupe section, or even the Big Bend —"

"Everythin' 'pears to be driftin' inter this section of late," a posseman interrupted in disgusted tones. "Most any day now I figger to see some of them there Inca fellers I read about once to be droppin' in from South America."

"Yuh might not be so far wrong at that," Woodard remarked cryptically.

"Here's the metal stacked over in this corner," exclaimed another posseman, who had been nosing about.

Sheriff Baylor contemplated the recovered ingots with satisfaction.

"Yuh know," he observed suddenly, "I've a notion them jiggers figgered to move this stuff off somewhere else in a jiffy. Otherwise they woulda buried it here or hid it in some way. They wouldn't have left it stacked here with the aparejos alongside it, like they was all set to load it up again. What do you think, Jim?"

"Appears to make sense," Woodard agreed.

"Well, let's get it set to pack back to town," said the sheriff. "We'll load these hellions onto their horses and take them along, too. The coroner will wanta set on 'em, I reckon. We'll put 'em on exhibition and mebbe somebody will recognize 'em and give us somethin' to go on toward runnin' down the rest of the outfit. Rec'lect, Owen Hartsook said there was seven of 'em altogether. That means three more of the sidewinders are maverickin' around somewhere yet, and there may be more. How's yore arm, Pete?"

"It'll do, now it's tied up," returned the wounded deputy. "Hurts some, but I reckon I can stand it. I'm okay to ride."

"Me, too," grunted the other wounded

posseman, "but I shore wish I had a cushion to tie onto my saddle."

"Uh-huh, yuh got plugged in the part yuh use most," the sheriff replied. "Well, yuh can take yore vittles from the mantelpiece for a spell. Do yuh good to stand up a little."

The mules and the owlhoots' horses were led from under the overhang and loaded up. With a last glance around, the posse set off down the mountain. They reached the Pasajero without mishap and headed for town.

A little later, as he and Woodard rode together to the rear of the others, Sheriff Baylor asked a question.

"How come yuh to figger where them hellions would pack the stuff, Jim, and how come yuh to know to get there?"

In answer, Woodard briefly recounted the happenings of the day he was drygulched on the trail and Mary Allison carried off to the cave.

"And I've a notion," he concluded, "that if I had really been done in under that bush, like they figgered me to be, Mary Allison would never have been seen or heard of again."

"Yuh mean yuh figger they woulda murdered a woman?" the sheriff asked incredulously.

"Either that or carried her off some-where," Woodard replied.

"They musta figgered on cashin' her in," mused the sheriff. "They couldn't have kept her hid."

"There are other countries besides Texas," Woodard remarked.

"But gettin' her out of the country woulda been some chore," the sheriff protested. "They couldn't expect to pack her down to *mañana* land without somebody knowin' about it. They woulda had the hull state up and pawin' sand. Every peace officer in Texas woulda been on their trail."

"Not necessarily," Woodard disagreed. "Yuh see, we would have disappeared sorta together."

The sheriff stared, then nodded his under-standing.

"Yuh mean folks woulda 'lowed you two went off together. Well," he added, glancing at the Range Rider's sternly handsome face, "that wouldn't have been such a far-fetched notion. Mary is a mighty purty gal, and a thing like that has happened before. Sorta what folks expect, and sorta like to figger happens, too — cowboy and purty gal ridin' off together. Yeah, I've a notion that's just what folks would have opined was what hap-pened. Jim, it looks like we're up against an outfit with savvy."

"Yes, they've got plenty of wrinkles on their horns, and they won't stop at anything," Woodard agreed. "But," he added grimly, "I've a notion they've slipped a few times of late. Owlhoots allus do, sooner or later, pertickler in little things — little things that add up big before the last brand is run."

Sheriff Baylor turned in his saddle to stare into Woodard's face.

"Jim," he asked in low tones, "just who the blazes are yuh, anyhow? I've a mighty strong notion yuh ain't just a chuck ridin' cowpoke."

"We'll have a talk together when we get to your office," Woodard replied. "I've a notion it's getting pretty close to showdown."

Some hours later, Woodard and Baylor sat alone in the office. The sheriff glanced expectantly at his companion.

Woodard was fumbling with a cunningly concealed secret pocket in his broad leather belt. He laid something on the table between them.

Sheriff Baylor stared at the object, which glittered in the lamplight. It was a gleaming silver shield, the feared and honored badge of the Cattleman's Association.

The sheriff stared at the shield with bulging eyes.

"A — a 'sociation man!" he stuttered at length. "Yuh're a 'sociation man!"

"That's right," Woodard admitted. "Captain Mort Quigley got yore letter and sent me over to have a look."

Sheriff Baylor continued to stare at the badge. Suddenly he leaped to his feet.

"And I've got yuh placed!" he exclaimed, his eyes glowing. "You're the Range Rider!"

"Been called that," Woodard admitted.

Sheriff Baylor stared in awe at the almost legendary figure whose exploits were the talk of the whole Southwest.

"The Range Rider!" he repeated. "The Range Rider — settin' right here in my office! Well, I should have knowed it. I was wondering why I didn't hear somethin' from Quigley. I might have knowed he wouldn't let me down. Have yuh figgered out who's responsible for the hell raisin' hereabouts?"

"Yes, I think I have," Woodard replied quietly, "but so far I haven't a bit of proof that would stand up in co'ht. I'm pretty sure I know who the man is at the head of the outfit, but so far I have very little to go on other than my own conclusions. He's a smart man, Sheriff, and one who's been around plenty. We've got to have him plumb hawgtied before we move, and when we do, we've gotta move sudden and fast. He's not

147

the ordinary brand of Border owlhoot. He's just as ornery and salty as any of them, but he's got what most of them lack — brains. And he knows how to use them. We've got to outsmart him, and that 'lows to be considerable of a chore."

"I figger he's got about as much chance as a wax dog chasin' a asbestos cat through hell, with the Range Rider on his trail," Sheriff Baylor declared with conviction.

Woodard smiled, his even teeth flashing startlingly white in his bronzed face.

"Nice of yuh to say so," he replied, "but that hellion is a long ways from being in the loop, and I've a notion he'll do some horning and tossing before the twine tightens on him."

12

The town buzzed with excitement over the recovery of the stolen ingots and the slaying of the four owlhoots. Sheriff Baylor was showered with congratulations.

One of the first to compliment him was Sime Price.

"A fine chore, Woll," declared the bank president. "A mighty fine chore. We're plumb proud of yuh."

"But it don't pay much," Baylor sarcastically reminded his friend. "Now if it had been four snorted-up swampers loafin' in front of a bank, I'd have collected twenty thousand pesos!"

Old Sime tugged at his collar, hemmed and hawed, met the amused gleam in Jim Woodard's eyes and made no direct reply.

Nobody was able to identify the slain owl-hoots. The opinion was strengthened that the outfit was one operating from south of the Rio Grande.

For several days, Woodard was busy with routine chores at the Bar A. Then one afternoon Mary Allison asked him to ride to town with her. Just as they were preparing to leave, Carter Renshaw rode up and stopped for a cup of coffee and a cigarette.

"Yuh did a mighty good job in connection with that stage holdup," he congratulated Woodard. "Sheriff Baylor gives yuh the credit for runnin' down those swabs. You sure laid them by the head. A few more like that and perhaps we'll have peace and fair weather in this section again."

Woodard nodded his appreciation, a peculiar light in his green eyes.

"May see yuh both in town tonight," Renshaw observed as he prepared to depart. "I aim to ride that way after I go over my north range."

"I'm going to spend the night in town," Mary said. "I have some shopping to do tomorrow morning. I suppose Jim will ride back to the spread tonight."

"That's right," Woodard agreed. "Want to get at the west range early tomorrow. I figger there are plenty of fat beefs holed up in the canyons over there. We can use them."

Nobody but the sheriff knew of the experience Woodard and Mary Allison had undergone on the Pasajero Trail. Baylor gave out that Woodard had noticed tracks leading to the mountain the day before and had merely followed a hunch in suggesting that the robbers might have made them and were using Coffin Mountain as a hole-up.

"I don't want to scare them away from that mountain — yet," Woodard told him.

"Yuh think they'd have the nerve to use that cave for a hole-up again, after what happened?" Baylor asked incredulously.

Woodard smiled slightly and shook his head.

"No," he said, "I don't; but I do figger they'll use that mountain again, at least once. I'm sure hoping so, anyhow. If they do, it'll give us our chance to drop our loop. I figger, too, that losing the loot from the stage holdup put a crimp in their plans, and that they will strike somewhere else soon.

Most every spread in the section is rounding up cows for shipping about now, and somebody is sure to get careless. Those hellions know everything that's going on in the section and take advantage of any slips. They'll bust loose somewhere soon, yuh can be sure of that."

After visiting with the sheriff and old Crane Allison, Woodard dropped in at the Rambler for a bite to eat. Preston Grimes was present, and nodded to him. Carter Renshaw had not yet put in an appearance. Nor did he show up before Woodard left for the spread.

Twilight was deepening when the Range Rider left town. Woodard rode warily, scanning each thicket and grove as he passed. He was taking no chances with the outfit pitted against him. They would strike, and strike hard, if opportunity afforded.

But nothing happened during the course of his ride. He reached the ranchhouse without incident, stabled his horse and entered the big living room. He lighted a lamp and settled himself comfortably in an easy chair to enjoy a last leisurely smoke before going to bed. Deftly he manipulated paper and tobacco. He was just raising the little white cylinder to his lips when abruptly he became conscious of an acrid, pungent smell that a chance draught, perhaps, had wafted to his nostrils.

The odor was unpleasant, being slightly reminiscent of scorched cheese, but holding an elusive familiarity that stirred the chords of his memory and seemed to recall a disagreeable happening.

For some moments he sat at a loss to identify the raw aroma. Then abruptly he sat bolt upright in his chair.

"Marihuana!" he muttered. "That's what it is. Somebody has been smoking marihuana in here, sure as blazes! Who could it have been? I'm sure for certain none of the boys use the darn stuff."

He wondered a moment if he could be mistaken. He was so puzzled that he got to his feet and slipped into the kitchen to see if the cook had perchance left something on the stove that had burned. But the big kitchen was spotless as usual. Nor did he notice the odor after leaving the front of the house.

Still puzzled, he retraced his steps to the living room. The odor was as strong there as before. He wandered around the room, trying to run it down.

Abruptly he paused. He was beside the closed door that led to the spare bedroom he occupied. Here the acrid smell was stronger than anywhere else in the room.

For long moments Woodard stood without sound or motion, listening intently. That someone had been smoking the narcotic within the building he was now positive. And he was just as certain that the odor seeped from behind the closed door of his sleeping room.

In men who ride much with deadly danger a constant stirrup companion there develops a subtle sixth sense that often warns of peril when none, apparently, is present. Jim Woodard had that sense very strongly developed. And now the voiceless monitor in his brain was clamoring for attention.

Woodard knew something of the effects of marihuana. For instance, how it tended to bring murderous propensities to the fore. He had known men to use the drug to build up a false courage, to fortify themselves in face of danger or to dull normal inhibitions. He knew that upon Mexicans and Indians in particular the effect was lethal where their impulses toward others were concerned.

"If some hellion is out to pull a killing, it would be just like him to take a whiff or two to nerve him up," he told himself. "I wonder, now, is some sidewinder holed-up in that room waiting for me to come in?"

He knew the owlhoot outfit operating in

the section would stop at nothing. They had already proven that. He realized also that by now they must consider him a menace that must be removed. As to whether they had divined his Ranger connections was doubtful, but his actions had shown conclusively that he was arrayed on the side of law and order or was playing some subtle game of his own. Neither was to their advantage. It was logical to believe that they would endeavor by every means possible to get him out of the way. One attempt at drygulching had failed. Doubtless the outfit was very much puzzled as to what had become of the two members who staged the attempt; but rather than deter them, the mystery would cause them to redouble their efforts. To plant a ruthless killer in his room to shoot him down as he entered would be a simple and easy way to eliminate him.

All this sped through his mind as he stood tense and silent outside the closed door, evolving a plan of action.

Careful not to make the slightest noise, he crept past the door and crouched against the wall. He loosened his guns in their sheaths, reached out and gently grasped the knob. The door opened outward. A swift turn of the knob, a hard jerk and he could fling it wide open. The unexpectedness of the happening would tend to throw off balance anybody hiding in the room and waiting for him to enter.

With one swift, supple movement, he put the thought into action. The door slammed open, banging against the wall.

There was a thundering crash, a gush of flame. Buckshot screeched through the opening. The window on the far side of the living room went to pieces with a prodigious smashing and clattering of broken glass. Smoke boiled from the bedroom.

Woodard went back along the wall a half dozen steps, guns out, his thumbs hooked over the cocked hammers. Every nerve strung to the tightness of stretched wire, he waited, his eyes trained on the door.

Nothing happened. The inner room was utter silence. He could hear the muffled shouts of the aroused cowboys in the bunkhouse. He waited for the thud of feet outside the bedroom that would tell the gun wielder was seeking to escape by way of the window; but no sound came to him.

His glance flickered past the open door and abruptly centered on a length of string dangling from the doorknob. Instantly he understood. Straightening up, he approached the open door and stepped boldly into the bedroom, and halted. He was staring into the twin muzzles of a sawed-off shotgun.

13

For tense moments, Woodard stood gazing at the blackened muzzles. The wicked weapon was lashed to one of the posts of his bed and trained on the door. A broken string, tied securely to the triggers and looped around the hammers, showed how the gun had been fired.

"String tied to the door knob," he muttered. "If I'd opened the door to step inter the room, as the hellion figgered I'd do, I'd have got both barrels dead center. If the sidewinder hadn't stopped to take a drag on a reefer before he started to work, that's just what would have happened. The owl-hoot brand allus slip up on the little things. Everything was lined up perfect, but he had to go and smell up the house with marihuana. Some outfit, though. This makes two tries. I'd better make it my business that there isn't a third time. The luck can't hold out forever."

The open window showed how the killer had gained entrance to the bedroom. He had doubtless left the same way, after rigging up his infernal machine.

Boots pounded on the veranda. An instant later the outer door banged open and the Bar A cowboys surged into the room, guns out and ready, old Stiffy leading the way. They took in the situation at a glance and swore explosive oaths as they examined the devilish contraption lashed to the bed post.

"We heard it let go," Stiffy said. "Didn't know what had busted loose, but figgered we'd better get here pronto. Reckon the hellion musta been keepin' tabs on the house. Saw you and Mary ride away and figgered it for his chance, when there was nobody here. Easy for him to slip in after it got dark and us fellers went to bed. Of all the pizenous, fangin' blankety-blank-blanks! Son, yuh shore had a close call. How come it didn't get yuh? Them muzzles are trained to down anybody who opened the door."

Woodard explained just what happened.

"Yuh got a keen nose, all right," said Stiffy, sniffing sharply. "I don't smell a thing."

"It's considerable drafty in here right now," Woodard replied, glancing at the smashed window. "The place got aired out in a hurry right after I opened the door."

"Nothin' would please me better'n to let air through the hyderphobia skunk that rigged up that contraption," growled Stiffy.

"Don't know what this section is comin' to. It ain't safe to be alive around here anymore. They're shore out to get yuh, son. Reckon they aim to even up for losin' them silver bars. If I was you, and had a outfit like that gunnin' for me, I'd trail my twine outa this section, pronto."

"Good advice," Woodard agreed. "But I'm not taking it."

"Didn't figger yuh would," grunted Stiffy. "But yuh're a plumb damn fool not to."

After examining the ground under the bedroom window, and failing to find any footprints, the cowboys went back to bed. Woodard sat in the living room for some time before retiring, thoughtfully smoking. Once he got up and walked to the smashed window. For some moments he stood gazing toward the unseen waters of the bay. His glance shifted to the dark bulk of Coffin Mountain shouldering the star-strewn sky, and back again to the southwest.

"Figger it won't be long, now," he mused. "The sidewinders are getting desperate. I've a notion they're purty bad scairt, and slipping up again tonight won't make them feel any better. Anyhow, we've thinned 'em out considerable. Those four the other night might make nine altogether, not counting the one I figger I winged the night I rode in here. I've a notion there wasn't more'n a dozen or so working this end of the game in the beginning. Figger the next move they make will bring out the leaders of the pack, short-handed as they must be. If things work out right, we'll drop a loop on the hull crawling nest of them. Sure hope I get a letter from Captain Mort tomorrow. A report on those specimens I sent to the State University would help, too."

His thoughts shifted to Mary Allison, whom he had left in town.

"Better ride up there fust thing in the morning," he decided. "Don't want to take any chances with her. No telling what the hellions are liable to pull."

Pinching out the butt of his cigarette, he extinguished the light and went to bed, the dumb muzzles of the sawed-off glaring through the dark over his head.

When he arrived at the Lorenzo post office the following morning, he found the hoped-for letter from Captain Quigley awaiting him. He read the contents with keen satisfaction, an exultant glow in his green eyes.

"Tying up," he muttered. "Everything tying up perfect. Just a loose end or two banging around yet, and I've a notion I'll hitch a knot in them mighty soon."

There was no report from the University laboratory as yet, but he had hardly expected it so soon and was not particularly disappointed at its nonarrival.

Mary Allison was much concerned when she heard what had taken place at the ranchhouse the night before. Woodard told her about it as they rode through the golden Autumn sunshine on the way back to the spread. For some time she sat her horse in silence, after he had finished. Suddenly she turned in her saddle and let the steady gaze of her wide blue eyes rest on his face.

"Jim," she said slowly, "as much as I hate to lose you, I think you had better give up your job and leave."

Woodard smiled down at her from his great height, his green eyes sunny as a summer sea.

"Why?" he asked.

"Because," she replied, "I'm afraid for you. Those outlaws hate you for what you have done to them. They'll try again, and the next time they may not fail. Yes, I think you had better go."

"Firing me?" Woodard asked, still smiling.

"You know very well I'm not," the girl replied. "I want you to leave for your own sake, not mine."

"Figger I'd leave yuh to fight it out alone?"

"No," she replied, "that's just what I'm afraid of, that you won't. But if you stay and something happens to you, I'll — I'll never forgive myself."

"Don't let it worry yuh, little lady," the Range Rider replied, abruptly grave. "It's other folks things are going to happen to — soon."

Glancing at his face again, she saw that his eyes were no longer the smiling blue-green of the sea warm in the sun. They were the ominous gray of that same sea under a wintry sky of storm driven clouds and icy wind. He was staring into the southwest, his face bleak, his mouth sternly set, and the girl felt that for the moment he had completely forgotten her presence.

After pausing at the ranchhouse for a helping of chuck, Woodard rode to the west range, where he found old Stiffy and the other hands busy combing out beefs from the brakes and canyons.

"Figger we can get a prime herd outa them holes," the grizzled puncher told him. "They're plumb fat and sassy and rarin' to go."

Two days later, Woodard again rode to town. He found the expected laboratory report awaiting him. He was greatly pleased with the contents.

"I was right," he told himself. "Just what I expected. Better even than I expected. Well, looks like the little lady won't hafta worry about that mortgage on her spread. No wonder those hellions were making such a play for it. And this ties up with everything else I suspected. All I need now is to drop my loop on the side-winger. I figger he'll make another move, and soon. That will be my chance. This is going to take some thinking out. Can't afford to make any slips, not with that outfit. One slip and he'll slide away like a snake inter a hole."

He left the post office and went to look for Sheriff Baylor, whom he found seated at his desk. He handed Baylor the folded sheet of paper in its envelope.

"Put this in yore office safe," he told him. "It's a chemical analysis of the land that makes up the Bar A's south range — that barren stretch along the bay. Hold onto this report until I ask for it. If for any reason I shouldn't ask for it, it goes to Mary Allison. The report speaks for itself and isn't hard to understand."

The sheriff took the paper wonderingly. He started to ask a question, but a glance at the Range Rider's face deterred him. With a nod, he opened the safe, stowed the paper in an inner compartment and locked the safe.

"Okay," he said. "It'll be there for yuh when yuh want it. And now have you figgered out anythin' else in connection with that nest of sidewinders."

"I've got something lined up," Woodard replied, "but it all depends on their making another move, which I figger they'll do before long. I'll be back day after tomorrow and tell yuh what I want done."

He paused for a word with old Crane Allison, who was stretched out on the bunk in his cell, and then rode back to the spread.

"We'll start up north on that west range and work down," he told Stiffy. "I figger we should be able to clean those canyons by the end of the week. Then we'll have another herd ready for shipping."

As he helped the Bar A hands comb the brakes the following day, Woodard was wondering where the owlhoots would strike next. He was fairly certain that they would strike, and before long. But he was totally unprepared for the move they did make.

14

It was mid afternoon, and Woodard and his men had combed a number of good beefs from a shallow draw in the western hills. Outside the draw they paused to breathe their horses and enjoy a smoke. Old Stiffy was holding out on the advantages of a "hooley-ann" in calf roping and a "mangana" for use in a pen.

"A good hand can throw a mangana from horseback as well as on foot," another waddie observed.

"When a cow has a good runnin' start, loopin' both fore feet is liable to throw him too hard and bust him all up," Stiffy maintained. "Now with a mangana de cabra —"

"Hell, ketch a cow around the neck and by both fore feet at the same time — and that's the only right way to use a *mangana de cabra* — and yuh're mighty nigh shore to bust a neck or a leg, if he happens to have got up speed," the other interrupted. "Give me a good straight underhand toss for mine any time. Loop the critter over the head and yuh got him, and less damage liable to be done."

"And if yore horse ain't plumb set, you are the one what's liable to get busted, not the cow," declared Stiffy. "Pertickler if yuh happen to be tied hard and fast."

"A good cowhand allus ties hard and fast," observed another rannie, starting an argument that is as old as the cow business.

"That's coverin' too much territory," Stiffy disagreed. "Up nawth they allus takes their dallies. Three, four loops around the horn, and turn go if yuh want to, and there's just as good cow chasers up there as there ever was in Texas. Now I rec'lect when I was ridin' for the Hashknife outfit in Montana —"

He paused suddenly in his harangue and stared northward.

"Say," he exclaimed, "some jigger has shore lit a big fire up there. What's he aimin' to do, barbecue a beef?"

The others followed the direction of his gaze. Smoke was rising from the brush a couple of miles or so to the north — a thick, dark column that broke under the force of the wind blowing steadily out of the north and spread out in a rolling cloud.

"That's too darn much smoke for a cookin' fire," somebody exclaimed. "Say, I wonder —"

Jim Woodard's voice rang out, hard, incisive.

"That's no cooking fire. That's a brush fire, and a big one. On yore toes, every one of yuh. The wind's rolling it along in this direction. It'll sweep these thorn pastures clear to the bay, and all the canyons on the way down. We gotta get the cows outa those

165

canyons before it gets here, and outa these pastures. Drive 'em south to the *sacaguista* flats by the water. Move, or we won't have enough beefs left on this spread to make steaks for a hummingbird!"

The cowboys were instantly alive to the danger that threatened. They tightened their cinches, gathered up the reins in a firm grip and made ready for hard riding.

"Three of yuh drive these cows we've rounded up, and beat through the pastures," Woodard directed. "Get everything yuh come across moving south. I figger it won't be much of a chore over there, with the smoke rolling this way ahead of the fire; but in the canyons and draws the darn fool critters will bore in deeper as the fire comes, and then they'll be goners. Come on, yuh work dodgers, the rest of yuh. That canyon half a mile to the south fust. Hightail!"

At top speed they raced for the canyon mouth, tearing through the thick brush, heedless of thorns and whipping branches. They pulled their horses to a skating halt at the dark opening of the gorge.

"One man stay here," Woodard directed. "Keep yore gun handy and fire a couple shots to warn us out when yuh rigger the fire's getting too close. All right, the rest of yuh. In we go!"

Up the canyon they thundered, urging their horses to greater effort.

"I figger it isn't over deep," Woodard shouted above the din of the pounding hoofs. "We'll ride to the head, then comb 'er to the mouth."

At the frowning end wall of the gorge they turned their horses and began beating the brush on the way back. As Woodard had surmised, there were a number of cows holed up in the canyon. They sent them down the gorge at breakneck speed. There was none of the careful handling customary to avoid running valuable fat off the beefs. With lashing quirts, wild yells and blazing six-shooters, they drove the bawling, terrified beasts before them. They were little more than two thirds of the way to the mouth when the two warning shots sounded.

"Touch and go," Woodard muttered. "If we get caught in one of these holes, it's curtains."

"Smoke's gettin' thick in here," bellowed old Stiffy. "She's roarin' ahead of that wind, all right."

Brands were showering down in the brush and the smoke was swirling in acrid clouds when they bulged from the canyon mouth. The fire was racing down from the north in a great sheet that seemed to stretch clear across the valley. The wind had strengthened and as far as they could see under the smoke clouds to the north was a seething inferno.

Once in the open, the cattle needed little urging to speed them southward. Woodard and his men rode in their wake until another canyon mouth was reached. They had gained considerably on the fire and the Ranger took a chance and entered the canyon.

Fortunately the gorge proved shallower than the first, but just the same the hand stationed at the mouth had pulled trigger twice before they cleared it with another batch of frantic cows.

The sun had almost set when they entered the third draw. A baleful reddish light slanted through the smoke clouds and the racing flames glowed brighter in the gloom.

"This one will be close," Woodard prophesied, "but we've got to take it."

The horses were beginning to show the effect of the wild afternoon. They were blowing and panting, their blood-congested eyes rolled, their nostrils flared. They were smeared with ash, scorched by falling brands, seared with sparks. The riders were in like case. But grimly they sped to the head of the draw, turned and tore back again through the thorny brush, spread out wide like an army in open order.

This time they were far up-canyon when they heard the distant shots that warned them to "git out and git out fast." They bulged from the gorge through a cloud of smoke and showering brands. Little flames raced through the grass, causing the horses to squeal with pain. Coughing, gasping, reeling in their saddles the cowboys managed to get the cows turned and headed south with the wall of flame at the very heels of their horses. The heat was terrific, the air almost unbreatheable with smoke. The falling brands were starting fresh flickers in the tinder-dry brush. And the *sacaguista* flats were still nearly three miles distant.

"There's one more that needs working," Woodard said. "Two men shove the cows along. The rest of yuh ride, and ride like yuh never did before. Let's go!"

Forcing their almost jaded horses to give their utmost, they raced southward. Woodard congratulated himself, that, in violation of his customary habit of not risking the sorrel's legs in ordinary range work, he was forking Rojo instead of one of the string that had been assigned to him when he took a job on the spread. Now in deference to the lesser ability of his companions' mounts, he was forced to hold the great horse in.

Overhead the lurid smoke pall reddened in the glare of the sunset. Streaks of fire that were burning brands whirled high on the wings of the roaring wind shot across its rolling surface. It was spangled with sparks. Bloody streamers coiled and writhed, throwing off opalescent glints. Sheets of what looked like living flame billowed forth. The north was an incandescent furnace. The salt flats were incarnadined. The bay was a sea of wine flecked with froth.

"If hell looks any wuss than back behind us, I don't wanta go there," grunted old Stiffy, glancing over his shoulder.

Woodard's teeth flashed white in his blackened face.

"If there's any slip-up in this canyon we're coming to, yuh got a good chance to find out," he said.

"Wish I'd led a better life," Stiffy replied. "Son, I'm plain scairt."

"Reckon a jigger who wouldn't be scairt of this mess would hafta have something plumb wrong with him," Woodard comforted. "Okay, here we go. You stay outside this time, Chuck. Yore cayuse is just about on his last legs."

The gloom was intense in the canyon. The

horses stumbled and lurched over the boulders, squealed wrathfully as the thorns tore at their hides. Cows could be heard popping the bushes. Others were lowing in a frightened manner.

"They know something is plumb wrong, but haven't got sense enough to get in the clear by themselves," Woodard said. "Okay, there's the end wall ahead — yuh can barely see it. Fan out and beat the brush."

"Get along little dogies, if yuh don't hanker to be roast beef afore yore time!" whooped Stiffy. "Yip-ay-ay!"

The previous experiences were repeated — a mad race with death under the blazing sky and through the inferno of smoke and heat. Lashing the terror-stricken cows with quirts and rope ends, the cowboys sent their staggering horses down the canyon.

"There's fire ahead of us!" one suddenly screamed. "And there's Chuck's shots!"

He was right. Directly ahead was a thin straggle of flame, started doubtless by a falling brand. It grew and heightened with terrifying speed. They could hear, above its crackle and roar, the reports of Chuck's six-shooter as he fired again and again. The cowboy was alive to his companions' danger and was frantically trying to warn them.

The cattle slowed as the sheet of flame

leaped before them. They tried to hang back, to shy away; but they were driven on by stinging blows and the banging guns in their ears. With mad bellows they charged through the fire. The cowboys, shielding their faces with their arms, rode after them.

Woodard felt the searing breath of the fire that leaped about him. His lungs were bursting. An iron band seemed to be tightening and tightening about his chest. His eyes were dazzled by the fierce light. He dared not breathe. He saw old Stiffy, who was riding next to him, reel in his hull, slump forward onto his horse's neck. He shot out a long arm and gripped the grizzled waddie as he was sliding to the ground.

The terrific strain of the sagging weight almost hurled Woodard from the saddle. He recovered his balance by a miracle of strength and agility, hauled the unconscious cowboy from his hull and draped his body across Rojo's withers. Stiffy's horse, freed of its rider's weight, shot ahead with a snort of relief. Woodard's voice rang out.

"Trail, Rojo, trail!"

The great sorrel, who had fallen behind the others, extended himself. His powerful legs shot backward like steel pistons. His iron beat the hard earth with a drumroll of sound. Snorting and blowing, he surged through the curtain of flame and thundered toward the canyon mouth, now only a few hundred yards distant. With a final explosive snort of relief he shot forth into the clearer air.

His appearance was welcomed by whoops of relief from the other hands, who, heedless of the fire roaring toward them from the north, were staring in horror up the smoke-filled gorge.

"Gosh, feller, we figgered yuh were both done in when Stiffy's horse came out with an empty saddle," exclaimed Chuck.

"Not this time," Woodard replied cheerily. "Stiffy'll come outa it in a minute. Heat and smoke got him. Roll 'em along. We just about got time to make the flats before our cayuses are plumb tuckered. Hightail, the wind is getting stronger."

The fire was roaring and crackling in the last thickets when they raced out upon the salt flats and into purer air. The horses stood with legs widespread, heads hanging, sides heaving, in the last stages of exhaustion. The cowboys tumbled out of their hulls and lay prone on the coarse grass. Woodard alone remained in his saddle, staring northward.

The scene was one of awesome beauty. East and west, the thorn pastures were a sea of flame, tossing, billowing, rolling and wavering in the wind. The cliffs to the west stood out in glaring relief, crimson with reflected light, ebon with shadows. Streamers of fire ran along the grass heads, leaping upward to the crest of a bush, diving into the hollows like shimmering serpents, writhing up the slopes, coiling, wavering, shot with opalescence, robed in scarlet, streaked with violet and purple and molten gold. Overhead the billowing smoke clouds were a reflection of the inferno below — a tossing, blinding tempest of fire.

Coffin Mountain was a blazing torch. Sheets of flame flowed up the slopes, climbing the tree trunks, bursting into skyrocket showers of sparks at their crowns. They went surging up adjacent ridges, vanished into canyons beyond, burst into view again, grander, brighter, more breathtaking. Skirmishing parties of fire were thrown out and went trailing their crimson spirals up farther ridges, turned black gorges into pits of brilliant light, climbed higher and higher, spread more and more, until the whole vast mountainside was webbed as if with a tangled network of lava streams.

For more than an hour Woodard sat entranced. But finally the fire burned itself out save for glows and smolders. The wind cleared the smoke from the sky somewhat, the stars came out, reddish and glowering. The moon came up from behind the eastern hills and hung above their crests like a deeply yellow orange poised on the edge of an inverted blue bowl. The bay turned darkly blue, then black, flecked with ghostly white, streaked with phosphorescent gleams.

Woodard shifted his gaze to the cattle dotted over the flats.

"We saved quite a few," he told his companions as he dismounted and rolled a cigarette.

"We lost plenty too, though," replied Stiffy, who had recovered his senses and was little the worse for wear. "I'm scairt this will be about the finish of the Bar A."

"The Bar A hasn't anything to worry about," Woodard said. "I'm sorry for the pore critters that got caught, but aside from that it doesn't mean a thing. The pastures will be all the better next year for this burning over, and there will be plenty of better cows grazing on them. Yuh don't hafta worry about a job, Stiffy."

"Well, Jim, if you say so, I'll borrow money to bet on it," the old cowboy replied simply. "I can't for the life of me understand how yuh figger it, but if you say it's so, I reckon it *is* so."

Woodard examined the cattle they had rescued. They were in prime condition, and made up a fine herd. They had recovered from their fright and were contentedly grazing, evidently considering the sparse grass of the flats better than nothing.

As they grazed, Woodard noted, they trended eastward, where the pasturage was better, and kept well bunched.

"They won't leave the flats to stray onto that burned-over section," he mused. "They'll stay right here for a spell."

For some time he sat his horse, gazing and thinking deeply. His face wore a pleased expression when he finally returned to his companions.

"Looks like she is about burned out," observed Stiffy. "Only a few flickers left here and there. I've a notion it's still purty hot up there yet, though. Chances are yuh could fry an egg on any rock in the trail."

"It'll cool down before long," Woodard told him. "A brush fire is allus hot as blazes for a time, but it doesn't hold up like it does where there is big timber. Those trees up on the mountain will smolder along for quite a while yet."

"A good rain will wash everythin' clean again," Stiffy said. "An them ashes will make fine fertilizer. I reckon if it wasn't for you, Jim, I'd be makin' purty good fertilizer myself about now."

"You'd pizen the grass roots," a companion declared. "And all the ant critters and things would get drunk on the red-eye that stewed outa yuh. Well, I shore hope she cools down soon. I could stand a mite of chuck about now. My stomach is wonderin' if I got my throat sewed up."

It was long past midnight, however, before they felt it was safe to ride north again. They found the ranchhouse and other buildings, set on a hill and away from the chaparral, untouched by the fire. Mary Allison, the cook and the wranglers were badly worried about their nonappearance.

"I don't care what else happened, just so you all got back safe," the girl declared in tones of heartfelt relief. "We didn't know what might have happened. It was terrible. How in the world do you imagine such a fire got started?"

"Isn't over hard to figger, I reckon," Woodard replied grimly. "It sure didn't catch by itself."

"You mean someone deliberately set it?"

"It didn't catch by itself," Woodard repeated.

"But why would anyone do such a thing?" the girl asked in bewilderment. "Who would profit by it?"

"I've a notion yuh'll find out all about that in time," Woodard replied. "Well, I figger after we eat, we'd all be better off for a mite of shuteye. It's been a sorta exciting day."

15

The following afternoon, Woodard prepared to ride to Lorenzo.

"How about them cows down on the flats?" Stiffy asked. "Reckon we'd better set a guard over 'em, hadn't we? There's some purty valuable critters down there."

Woodard answered promptly. "No, I don't want a guard set," he replied. "Leave them just as they are, and don't worry about them."

The old rannie looked bewildered. "It don't make sense to me," he declared dubiously. "But okay, if you say so."

Upon arriving at Lorenzo, Woodard immediately went to the office of Sheriff Woll Baylor.

"I figger we're set for the showdown," he told the old peace officer. "I calc'late that herd down on the flats will be a temptation the hellions won't be able to resist. It's sure for certain they're keeping tabs on everything we do, and when they see that herd is left unguarded, it's just about certain they'll make a play for it. If they do, I figger we'll have a mighty good chance to drop a loop on the hull outfit."

"Yuh mean we'll hole up outa sight and wait for 'em to come to run off the herd?"

Woodard shook his head.

"Not exactly," he said. "I want them to grab off that herd without any trouble. Now here is what I want yuh to do, Sheriff. This thing has got to be handled mighty careful so they won't catch on a trap is being laid for them. I've a notion they are mighty suspicious about now. They'll make sure everything is safe before they make a try for the beefs. It won't be hard for them to get a line on that, but I've a notion they haven't the least idea we'll do what we're going to do. Listen careful, now, and no slips. It may seem sorta loco to you, but I know what I'm doing."

Dusk was falling when Woodard rode out of Lorenzo. He stopped at the Rambler first and had a drink and a bite to eat. Preston Grimes was not in evidence at the moment. Nor did he see anything of Carter Renshaw or his foreman.

The night was dark, for the moon would not rise for some hours. Woodard made good speed along the shadowy trail, confident that his movements could not be observed. He rode several miles, until he reached the east end of the long hogback north of Coffin Mountain. Here he abruptly turned from the trail and took up a position at the edge of a thicket, where the shadows were deep. Dismounting, and allowing Rojo to graze, he smoked comfortably and waited.

An hour passed, and he heard the hoofbeats of an approaching horseman. A few minutes later Sheriff Baylor pulled off the trail and approached the thicket.

"Okay," Woodard told him. "The other boys all set?"

"They slid outa town in different directions, after dark," the sheriff replied. "There's my two deputies, the two fellers who rode with us the day of the stage robbery, and three other gents who can be counted on to stand up to anything that comes along. Yuh figger that'll be enough?"

"Nine," Woodard counted. "Sure, that'll be plenty. I doubt if there'll be more than that against us, and we'll have all the advantage of surprise on our side. I figger there'll be a shindig, though. At least three of those hellions aren't the sort to give up easy. We can't take any chances, Baylor, or we'll lose men. It's a salty outfit."

"They done proved that," grunted the sheriff. "Listen, ain't that somebody comin' down the trail? Two of 'em. That had oughta be the deputies, Pete and Cary. They were to get together up the trail a piece."

Less than an hour later, the full posse rode swiftly southward along the Pasajero. They were grim-faced and quiet, and sternly resolved.

To the very edge of the bay, Woodard led them. Then he turned sharply westward to follow the coastline. As he rode he continually glanced northward toward where Coffin Mountain loomed grim and massive against the stars. They were almost to the deep, land-locked cove he had discovered during his previous ride across the desert, when he saw what he expected and hoped to see.

On the dark crest of the mountain flickered a tiny light that swiftly grew in size. It flared and wavered, billowed high into the air, burned fiercely for a few moments, then quickly sank and died.

"There's the signal," Woodard said quietly. "Everything is all set. They're grabbing off the herd and shoving it along. Hightail, now. We haven't time to get in the clear."

The desert was deathly silent, shimmering faintly in the dim starshine. Butte and chimney rock stood out black and ominous. The hoofs of the horses made practically no sound in the soft sand as they flitted, wraith-like, through the gloom. Only the popping of saddle leather and the jingle of bridle irons betrayed them as flesh and blood and not ghostly mirages of the wasteland.

Woodard strained his eyes ahead. He exclaimed with satisfaction when the level shoreline began to slope gently upward. He knew they were approaching the deep, land-locked cove he sought. He veered Rojo slightly to the north and they skirted the cove some distance from the water's edge.

The slope of the land to the west was more abrupt than to the east. The crest of the sag was an outcropping of spired and broken rock which afforded the posse ample concealment. The horses were tethered in a straggle of thicket some distance down the slope, where a chance snort or stamping would not be heard. Tense and alert, the possemen took up positions of vantage and waited. The curve of the cove lay not more than a score of yards below where they crouched.

For a long time nothing happened. Then from out on the black waters of the bay came a sound, faint at first, but steadily loudening, a creaking and slatting, and the rustle and surge of something through the water.

"A straight hunch," Woodard breathed to the sheriff. "Here she comes."

In the mouth of the cove suddenly loomed something dim and enormous. Another moment and the watchers saw that it was a vessel of considerable size slowly entering the cove. Her square-rigged sails blotted out the stars, her hull was a huge blacker shadow against the black water.

Slowly she plowed forward with slatting canvas and creaking cordage. A sharp word of command sounded from her shadowy deck. The spreading sails were furled by unseen hands. There was a rattle of anchor chain through the hawsepipe, the splash of the hook in the water. The vessel swung on her cable and came to a halt, her bowsprit thrusting out parallel to the low bank.

Now that the ship was safely in the landlocked cove, her crew made no pretense of concealment. Lanterns were lighted and strung low in the rigging making the deck bright as day. She was revealed as a good sized coastwise vessel, broad of beam, bluff-bowed. Two-thirds of her spacious deck was converted into a corral by means of stout planks nailed to posts let into the deck boards.

The crew, Woodard counted a half dozen of them, moved about chattering together, sometimes in English, sometimes in Spanish. They cast expectant glances shoreward, opened the swinging gates of the corral on the deck, removed a portion of the deck rail and let down wide gangplanks that sloped gently from the deck to the shore. Then they lounged about, smoking, very much at their ease and apparently with no feeling of insecurity.

"Gosh, what a system!" breathed Sheriff Baylor. "So this is how they do it. Load 'em onto a ship and smuggle 'em inter Mexico or some place. Well, this is a new wrinkle in wideloopin'! Listen, don't I hear somethin'?"

Woodard heard it, too — the wail, thin with distance, of a tired and peevish steer.

"Get set," he whispered. "Here they come. Let 'em all get on board and then rush 'em."

The bleating of the approaching cattle grew louder. A soft rustling sound was heard, the swishing and sucking of many hoofs in the sand. The shipmen knocked out their pipes, became alert. They strung along the landward rail, peering and pointing.

Over the eastern hills, the upper circle of the late moon was just appearing. Objects became dimly visible. Far to the east shadowy shapes appeared, swiftly growing larger. The protests of the harried cattle sounded loud on the still air. Soon the herd could be clearly seen, and the horsemen who urged them on. Woodard counted four altogether.

Up to the cove raced the herd, slowing gradually. Two horsemen rode alongside their flanks and veered the leaders. They jostled and milled for a few moments, then, as the riders slashed them with quirts, turned onto the gangplank and thudded up it. They clattered across the deck, bawling protest, and were shoved through the corral gate. Soon the deck was packed with the bleating, jostling mass. The shipmen hurled trusses of hay into the enclosure and the cows gradually settled down to feeding.

When the last of the beefs were up the gangplank, the four horsemen dismounted and climbed to the deck, mingling with the shipmen. A swarthy, bearded giant of a fellow with gold rings in his ears came forward with a word of greeting.

"Okay," Woodard told his men. "Up and at them!"

The possemen rose to their feet and raced noiselessly down the slope. They were halfway up the gangplank before they were observed by the men on the deck. They whirled about with shouts of alarm. The light of the lanterns fell full on their faces.

One was a squat, broad-faced individual. His two companions were tall and broad-shouldered. They were Peaseley Wallace, the Double R foreman, Preston Grimes, and Carter Renshaw.

Jim Woodard was in the van of the charging possemen. His face was bleak as carved granite, his eyes coldly gray. On his broad chest gleamed the shield of the Association Riders. His voice rang out, edged with steel.

"In the name of the State of Texas! You are under arrest!"

Preston Grimes yelled a curse. His right hand flickered to his shoulder holster. Woodard drew and shot him between the eyes before he could clear leather. The roar of guns filled the air.

And now set in a fell and fierce fight. The crash of shots, the thudding of blows, the screams of wounded men, the bawling of terrified cattle rose in a wild pandemonium of horrific sound. Knives flashed, guns blazed. The owlhoots fought like cornered rats, as hopeless and as vicious. The giant captain of the smuggling crew, wielding a huge machete, rushed forward and fell with his face almost against the flaming muzzle of Sheriff Baylor's gun. A sailor closed with a posseman and the two crashed to the deck locked in a death grip. Woodard saw Peaseley Wallace's barrel line with his breast, but before the foreman could pull trigger, Woodard's Colt bucked in his hand. Wallace fell backward with a choking cry.

Carter Renshaw leaped forward, his gun blazing. Woodard weaved to one side, pulled trigger and heard the hammer of his six click on an empty shell.

Renshaw's gun was also empty. He slashed a wicked blow at the Range Rider's head with the barrel. Woodard ducked it and the two crashed together, dropping their empty guns. Back and forth across the blood-slippery deck they struggled, tearing, straining, jolting one another with short, wicked blows. Renshaw was nearly as tall as the Range Rider, and many pounds heavier, and he seemed to be made of steel wires. Twice his greater weight and giant strength had Woodard nearly down, and twice his own greater youth and skill saved the Range Rider. On the very edge of the yawning open hatch they strained and wrestled, neither giving an inch. Renshaw had a grip on Woodard's throat with one hand and the Range Rider gasped for breath as the fingers tightened and dug into his flesh. He struck at Renshaw's face with his free hand, but the other ducked his head against his opponent's shoulder and doggedly held on.

Woodard felt his strength going. He could not resist for long the throttling of that murderous grip. With a mighty effort he leaped backward, Renshaw's nails furrowing his flesh as his fingers slipped. Woodard staggered drunkenly, scant feet from the open hatch, breathing in great gulps. Renshaw, his face like a madman's, his eyes glaring murder, rushed at him with clutching hands.

Woodard ducked under the grip, caught Renshaw by the thighs and hurled him over his shoulder — helped as much by Renshaw's own mad rush as by the trained strength of the heave.

Renshaw hurtled through the air, arms and legs revolving. With an awful cry of agony and despair he shot down the open hatch. The cry was abruptly stilled by the crash of his broken body on the timbers far below.

Gasping and choking, red flashes storming before his eyes, Woodard sagged against the mast, fighting the waves of blackness that threatened to engulf him. Dimly he realized that the sounds of conflict had stilled. The deck was littered with bodies and drenched with blood. Over against the rail, several possemen were binding two of the smuggling crew who still remained on their feet.

Sheriff Baylor came striding across the deck, mopping at the blood that streamed down his face.

"Two of the boys won't ride back with us," he said somberly. "Pete has a busted arm. McGregor got a hunk of meat scalloped off his ribs. Evans has a knife wound in his back, not bad, I figger. All the sidewinders are dead, except them two water snakes the boys are tyin' up over there. It was some shindig. You all right, son?"

"I'll be all right soon as I get my wind back," Woodard replied.

"I saw you and Renshaw goin' to it — who'd have believed he'd be mixed up in such a business? But I couldn't get over to help yuh. You handled him all right by yoreself, though."

"I don't want to tackle another like him," Woodard replied. "For a while it was touch and go as to who would go down the hatch. Well, I guess this about winds up the hull business. Let's look things over."

"They were working it comin' and goin'," the sheriff reported a little later. "The cabin is stuffed full of dobe dollars, bales of marihuana, and other contraband. Looks like

189

we've busted up a smugglin' ring as well as a wideloopin' outfit."

"Reckon they went in for most everything," Woodard agreed. "Renshaw wasn't the ordinary owlhoot variety by a long ways. He was a mighty smart hombre. Too bad he couldn't have put his smartness to some good use. I calc'late he would have gone a long ways."

"How in blazes did yuh ever get a line on Renshaw?" the sheriff wondered. "He's the last jigger in the section I'd have figgered as wearin' the owlhoot brand. I don't reckon anybody hereabouts ever suspected him of anythin' off-color."

"Tell yuh all about it tomorrow," Woodard replied. "Right now we'd better be headin' back to town with the prisoners, and to get the boys patched up. Leave two men here to look after the ship and those cows. I'll tell the boys up at the spread to ride down here tomorrow and run 'em back where they belong. I reckon the customs authorities will take over the ship. It's sorta in their line, seeing as she was engaged in smuggling."

A little later the possemen rode off with their captives, taking with them also the bodies of the slain special deputies. Where the Pasajero passed the Bar A ranchhouse,

Woodard pulled up.

"See yuh tomorrow, Sheriff," he told Baylor. "I want to bring Mary Allison along with me. There are several things she'll be interested in hearing, and I figger she'd oughta be there when her dad gets outa jail."

"Along with everythin' else, yuh gonna show Crane Allison didn't kill Ward Grimes?" asked the startled sheriff.

"Reckon so," Woodard smiled. "He sure didn't kill him — pity he didn't. Grimes had lived too long as it was. He served a useful purpose by hanging on a spell, though. Gave me one of my fust leads on Carter Renshaw."

16

Woodard and Mary Allison rode to Lorenzo together the following afternoon. As if to celebrate the return of peace and order to the section, the Nueces country was showing what it could do in the way of a perfect day. The autumn sun poured down a flood of gold. A mystic purple haze swathed the hills, softening and mellowing the crags and pinnacles until even grim Coffin Mountain was a vision of loveliness robed in violet and crowned with light. No branch moved in the still air, no grass blade rustled. The sky above was tenderest blue, deepening to lilac edged with saffron along the thin, fine line of the horizon.

Woodard wore the silver shield of the Association Riders. His green eyes were sunny. He sat his great red-golden horse with careless grace.

Mary Allison's bright hair was a smoldering glory in the sunlight. On her piquant little face was an expression of quiet happiness, but there was a slightly wistful look in her wide blue eyes.

Lorenzo was seething with excitement when they arrived in town. Men stood in groups and stared at the tall form of the Range Rider as he rode past.

In front of the bank building, Woodard pulled Rojo to a halt.

"Wait a minute," he told Mary. "I got a chore to do."

He dismounted, strode up to the building, ripped the reward notice from its fastening and tore it across twice. Then he entered the bank. Heedless of the stares of the bank employees, he crossed the outer room to Sime Price's private office and flung the door open.

The bank president looked up, decidedly startled, as Woodard entered. The Range Rider walked up to his desk and flung the torn reward notice upon it.

"Why — why — what does this mean?" gulped Price.

"It means," Woodard told him sternly, "that yuh're not offering any more rewards for dead bank robbers. Law enforcement is going back into the hands of the proper officers."

Old Sime started to swell like a spring bullfrog, but the look in Woodard's eyes struck the words unuttered from his lips.

"Get yore hat and coat and come along with me to the sheriff's office," Woodard ordered.

"Yuh — yuh mean I'm under arrest?" quavered Price.

Some of the sternness left Woodard's face. His lips quirked slightly at the corners.

"Nope," he said. "Mebbe yuh ought to be, but yuh're not. Yuh're going there to listen to some things. And before yuh're finished," he added grimly, "I've a notion yuh're going to be sweating more than yuh are now. Get going."

Old Sime "got going," without protest. With Woodard towering beside him, leading Rojo, he walked up the street to Sheriff Baylor's office. Woodard gestured him to enter, and paused to help Mary dismount. He and the girl went up the steps together. Woodard nodded to Baylor, and to old Crane Allison, who was with the sheriff at his desk, placed a chair for Mary and sat down. With a gleam of amusement in his green eyes as he surveyed the expectant group, he deftly rolled a cigarette and lighted it.

"Well, I'm ready to answer yore question of last night, Sheriff," he said. "I fust got to thinking about Carter Renshaw because of the way in which he walked."

"The way he walked!"

Woodard nodded, and puffed on his cigarette.

"That's right. Renshaw was particular to intimate that he had been a cattleman over in the Big Bend country all his life. He'd been a cowman in the Big Bend, all right, but he had also been a deep water sailor, and for a number of years. I noted his walk fust off. He had the walk of a man who had spent a lot of time on the deck of a ship. He had what's called the 'sailor's roll.' I really didn't think anything of it at fust; but later on, when I learned more about him, I realized that he made it a point never to mention anything about his seafaring. That made me wonder. Besides, I'd already started wondering about him because of something else."

He paused, regarding his cigarette with a

contemplative eye. His hearers sat tensely expectant.

"Rec'lect, Sheriff," he continued, "the morning Ward Grimes was found to have died in Doc White's office? Renshaw, when he came here to tell Allison the news, mentioned that he had been with Grimes the night before and had left him, to all appearances, well on the road to recovery. I reckon Grimes was well on the road to recovery when Renshaw dropped in to see him, but when Renshaw left, closing the door of his room and telling Doc that Grimes was asleep, Grimes was dead."

"Yuh mean to say Renshaw killed him?" exclaimed Crane Allison.

"He did," Woodard replied.

"But Doc White said Grimes died of nacherel causes — a thrombosis, I think he called it."

"Yes, that's what Doc believed," Woodard nodded. "But he was wrong. Doc had no reason to believe otherwise, and he certainly had no reason to think Carter Renshaw might have been responsible for Grimes' death."

The sheriff shook his head in bewilderment.

"How in blazes did you catch on?" he asked.

Woodard smiled, and paused to roll another cigarette.

"Remember me asking Doc if there was anywhere in town I could buy peaches? And Doc said there wasn't a peach in town at that time of the year. Well, when I stepped into the room where Grimes' body lay, I distinctly smelled the odor of peach blossoms. As it happens, hydrocyanic acid, one of the deadliest and swiftest poisons known, smells like peach blossoms. The odor is unusual, and distinctive. And hydrocyanic stops the heart and leaves outward symptoms similar to those resulting from death by thrombosis. Renshaw was the last person to see Grimes alive. When he entered that room, he undoubtedly carried a vial of hydrocyanic acid with him. He managed somehow to give Grimes a drop or two, or a good whiff of the gas — that's all that would be necessary to cause death."

"But why would he want to kill Grimes?" asked the bewildered sheriff.

"Because Grimes was a weak sister, despite his setting up to be a salty hombre," Woodard replied. "Allison gunning him up broke his nerve completely. Renshaw evidently decided he had to be done in, for safety's sake. He knew too much, and wasn't to be trusted. Most of Renshaw's outfit were cold propositions, but he slipped on Grimes, just like he slipped on that drunken deputy marshal over to Dynham."

"Grimes was sorta different from his brother," remarked the sheriff.

Woodard smiled slightly.

"Grimes never had a brother, so far as I was able to learn," he replied. "Preston Grimes, so called, was not his brother but one of Renshaw's bunch playing the part. I got suspicious of Preston Grimes when he and Renshaw made such a strong play of not getting along. That row between Peaseley Wallace and Preston Grimes in the Rambler was a phony if there ever was one. When a gent reaches for a gun and aims to use it, he doesn't pull it straight up from his holster, with the muzzle pointing to the floor. He drags it back, with the business end trained on the gent he aims to down. Wallace pulled his gun straight up and let Grimes get the drop on him. That set me thinking about Grimes. So I wrote to Captain Quigley and he got in touch with the bank over in Louisiana from which Preston Grimes was supposed to have brought his credentials. The bank wrote back they never heard of such a person. The credentials were forged, of co'hse, to enable Preston Grimes to get hold of the Rambler, a valuable property."

"And Ward Grimes really did murder my son, then?" asked Crane Allison.

"He did," Woodard replied, "to get the reward money offered for dead bank robbers. When Price put up that reward notice, and the other bankers in the section followed suit, Renshaw, who never missed a chance to cash in on things, saw a good opportunity to pick up some easy money. Tom Allison was one of the victims, just as that pore devil of a miner over to Dynham was, and the two Mexicans at Armstrong. Those two hellions locked up in the cells will testify to that. Grimes followed Tom Allison into the bank and shot him down in cold blood."

"How do yuh know that?" Sime Price interpolated in feeble protest. "Allison did come inter the bank and demand money."

Woodard smiled, a smile that had little of mirth in it.

"He did, because he had every reason to think he had a right to," he replied. "Being two-thirds drunk, he acted queer and awkward. Tom Allison came inter the bank to get a check cashed."

"To get a check cashed!"

In answer to the exclamation, Woodard

drew a soiled blotter from his pocket. He handed it to the sheriff, gestured Price to help the peace officer examine it.

"Yuh'll notice it has been used but once," he said. "See if yuh can read what's on it."

The sheriff laboriously traced the blurred, inverted impressions with his forefinger.

"Looks like a one, and a coupla naughts up here," he muttered. "Uh-huh that's what it is, 'cause right below it is 'one hundred' spelled out. And there's somethin' else before them figgers up above. I can't make out the fust word. It's all blurred. But the second one — 'A — 1 — 1 —' By gosh! it's 'Allison,' that's what it is!"

"Yes," Woodard said quietly. " 'Pay to the order of Tom Allison $100.00' is how the first line, printing and writing, would read. This is the blotter Ward Grimes used to blot the check he gave Tom Allison in the back room of the Rambler. What Allison was reaching for when he was shot was not a gun, but the check he had in his pocket.

"Catch on, Price?" he asked the white-faced banker.

"Everything was tying up, yuh see," Woodard continued. "I'd already placed Renshaw as a man with seafaring experience. Also I had about decided that the cows wide-looped from this section were being taken out by way of the sea. There was really no place else for them to go. It was ridiculous to figger the wideloopers were running herd after herd clean across the desert to Mexico. That flare on top of Coffin Mountain was undoubtedly a signal fire. What else but to notify the smuggling ship standing off shore to put in for a load? One of the owlhoots we downed when they made the try for Slim Dryden's shipping herd was packing a box of snuff, a strange thing for a cowhand to be carrying, but a favorite type of eatin' tobacco with seamen.

"Most of the owlhoots that had been cashed in were Apaches or Apache breeds, something rarely seen this far east. Renshaw came here from the Big Bend, and brought his hands with him. The Big Bend and on west is Apache country. Renshaw brought the breeds from there, too. Part of an outfit he worked with over there, according to what the prisoners we have said. He never used his regular ranch hands in his owlhoot business. I doubt if most of them even know anything about it. That way he avoided anything that might tie him up with what was going on.

"Also, he had ready access to all that was taking place in the section. He was at Dryden's place playing poker the night before

Dryden corralled his shipping herd in that canyon. Of co'hse he learned about it while he was at Dryden's place. He knew all about the Bar A herds. He knew about the silver ingots secretly shipped by way of the Dynham stage. He was a solid citizen with connections and was in a position to learn things."

"That's right," put in Sheriff Baylor. "I rec'lect him speaking about what the Dynham stage packed the day he came in to raise hell about one of his herds being wide-looped."

Woodard nodded, and reached for his tobacco.

"Yes, he pretended to lose stock, too, of co'hse. That was part of his cover-up game. Chances are he did have his hellions run off some cows from his place. He didn't stand to lose anything, having a ready sale for them. He just shipped 'em by water instead of rail, and that fooled the honest hands he had working for him. He had plenty of savvy, all right.

"What gave me my first line on why he wanted the Bar A spread was the way he spoke Spanish. The day Mary and I were drygulched on the Pasajero Trail, a Mexican came into the Rambler and spoke to Renshaw in Spanish. Renshaw replied in the same language, but he didn't speak the kind of Spanish the Mexican spoke — the kind of Spanish that is spoken in Mexico. He spoke much purer Spanish, but not quite Castilian. He used the kind of Spanish spoken by the people of Chile and Peru. He had doubtless been in Chile in the course of his wanderings over the world, had spent considerable time there, enough to learn the language, and learn it well."

"But why did he want my ranch?" asked Mary Allison. "It is not as good a spread as the Double R."

Woodard smiled at the girl.

"No, it is not as good a spread for cattle raising, but it is a heap more valuable."

He turned to Sheriff Baylor.

"Fetch me that paper out of the safe," he said.

Baylor complied with the request. Woodard spread the paper on the sheriff's desk.

"After Preston Grimes bought the Bar A mortgage from the Lorenzo bank, I did some hard thinking," he said. "I knew right then that there was something valuable on the Bar A. The question was, what and where? Most of the spread was regulation rangeland; but the salt flats down by the bay are different. It is an unusual stretch of land down there, a rather unique geological

202

formation. I got curious about that land and did a little investigating. I saw that the terrain is strikingly similar to the great nitrate deposits in Chile. I took some specimens and sent them to the State University to be analyzed. The report states that the land is very rich in nitrates, the percentage considerably higher even than the world-famous Chilean deposits. Renshaw had been to the Chile nitrate fields. He understood the worth of the Bar A deposit and set out to get control of it. It was his big chance. He could tie onto the Bar A, get rid of his owlhoot connections, just as he got rid of Ward Grimes, and set up as a prosperous, respectable citizen. He might have gotten by with it, if, like the owlhoot brand allus does, he hadn't slipped up in a few little things."

"Nitrates," repeated Crane Allison. "What are they good for?"

"They're used to make fertilizer, explosives, and other things of commercial value," Woodard replied. "That deposit is, of co'hse, not nearly as large as the ones in Chile, but it's not small and is conveniently located for transportation to market. It won't make you a millionaire, Allison, but it will put yuh in mighty comfortable circumstances and backlog yuh against bad seasons and so on."

Woodard paused, smiling at his listeners.

The silence was broken by old Sime Price, who had been sitting with his head in his hands. Abruptly he straightened up and spoke.

"I done wrong about them infernal reward notices," he said. "I meant well, but I reckon I done wrong."

Crane Allison got to his feet. He walked over and placed a gnarled hand on the banker's bowed shoulders.

"I reckon we all do wrong, at one time or another, Sime," he said gently. "Anyhow, it takes a honest man with guts to stand up and admit he has made a mistake. I don't hold anythin' against yuh, Sime, and here is my hand on it."

The two old men shook hands, looking into each other's eyes.

"Well, I reckon that's about all," said Sheriff Baylor, bustling from behind his desk. "I'm goin' over and see Judge Wheeler. I 'low the judge will fix up the papers pronto. Crane had oughta be turned loose by tomorrow mornin' at the latest."

Woodard stood up, stretching his long arms above his head, and smiled down at them from his great height.

"Yes, I reckon that's about all," he repeated Baylor's words. "Time I was riding.

Captain Mort will have another little chore lined up for me by the time I get back to the post. I'll start now. It's cooler out on the desert at night."

Mary Allison also rose. "I'll ride with you as far as the Bar A," she said.

They rode out of town together. The sunset was flaming scarlet and gold over Coffin Mountain when Woodard pulled his great sorrel to a halt before the ranchhouse. He sat smiling down at the bright-haired girl beside him. Her wide blue eyes gazed up into his.

"Will — will I see you again?" she asked.

Woodard smiled. "An Association man rides a long trail, little lady," he said. "A long trail, and a lone one. But even the longest trail comes to an end sometime. So I won't say *'adios,'* but *'hasta luego.'* "

" 'Till we meet again,' " Mary Allison translated. "We'll let it go at that." Then, in soft tones, she gave him the farewell with which the folks of Mexico speed the well loved departing one on his way.

"*Vaya usted con Dios!* Go you with God!"

Once, far down the old Trail of the Travelers, he turned and waved his hand. Then the watching girl saw him face to the front, square his shoulders and ride on into the sunset, tall and graceful, atop his great red-golden horse, to where there was work to be done and danger and adventure waited!